CW01507522

Copyright © 2025 by Helen Middle

Contents

Chapter One

THE SHOP HAD BEEN quiet for days. Clara Wren stood behind the counter and listened to the ticking. Dozens of clocks lined the shelves, their hands moving in patterns she knew by heart. Some ticked fast, some slow, but they all measured time in their own way. The sound should have been comforting. Instead, it reminded her of everything that was slipping away.

She wiped a smudge from the glass counter with her apron. The shop window behind her was coated with Birmingham soot. It made the afternoon light look grey and tired. Passers-by hurried along the street outside, their footsteps quick against the cobbles. None of them stopped. None of them looked in.

The shelves that once held rows of pocket watches and timepieces now sat mostly empty. Her father had sold the stock bit by bit over the past year. What remained were the broken watches waiting for repair, the tools of the trade, and the fading name painted above the door. Wren's Watch Repairs. It had been her grandfather's shop first, then her father's. Now it was hers to keep alive, even if nobody knew it.

Clara glanced at the ceiling. Above her, in the small bedroom, her father would be sleeping. Or trying to. The cough that woke him in the night had grown worse these past weeks. Dr Morrison said there was nothing to be done except rest and warmth. Rest they could manage. Warmth cost coal, and coal cost money they didn't have.

She pushed the thought aside and turned to the workbench tucked in the corner behind the counter. A pocket watch lay there, its case open, its insides exposed. The customer had brought it in three days ago. A merchant's son with soft hands and a loud voice. He had looked at Clara as if she were a parlour maid.

"I need this repaired," he had said. "Where's Mr Wren?"

"My father is unwell," Clara had replied, keeping her voice steady. "I can help you."

The young man had frowned. "I'll leave it, but I want it done properly. Tell your father I'll be back Friday."

Clara had nodded and taken the watch. She had not mentioned that her father's hands shook too much to hold the tools anymore.

Now she sat on the tall stool and pulled the watch closer. The workbench lamp cast a circle of light over the brass casing. She picked up her father's magnifying glass and peered inside. One of the gears had slipped out of place. The spring was overwound. It would take patience and care to fix, but she had both.

Her father had taught her everything. Not because he thought a woman should learn the trade, but because she had wanted to learn. She had been seven years old when she first climbed onto his lap and watched him work. His hands had been steady then, his voice calm as he explained how each tiny piece fit together.

"A watch is like a heart," he had told her. "Every part depends on the others. If one fails, the whole thing stops."

Clara had loved the way the pieces gleamed under the light. She had loved the satisfying click when a gear slid into place. Most of all, she had loved the silence that came after, when the watch began to tick again.

She picked up a pair of tweezers and carefully lifted the loose gear. Her hands were small, which made the work easier. She had calluses on her fingertips from years of handling tools. Ink stains marked her right hand where she gripped the pen to write invoices. They were not the hands of a lady, but they were skilled.

The gear slipped back into position with a soft click. Clara adjusted the spring tension and checked the balance wheel. Everything looked right. She closed the case and wound the watch. The ticking started up, steady and strong. She smiled.

A violent cough broke the silence. Clara's head snapped up. The sound came from upstairs, harsh and rattling. She set the watch down and hurried to the door behind the counter. The narrow stairs creaked under her feet.

Her father's room was at the top. It was small, with a single window that overlooked the alley. The bed took up most of the space. Her father lay there, propped up on pillows, his face pale against the linen. He was thin. Too thin. His nightshirt hung loose on his shoulders.

"Papa?" Clara crossed to the bed and sat on the edge. She poured water from the jug on the bedside table into a cup and held it to his lips.

He drank a little, then pushed it away. "I'm all right," he said, his voice rough. "Just a cough."

"You should rest."

"I've been resting for weeks." He tried to sit up straighter and winced. "How is the shop?"

Clara hesitated. She could tell him the truth. That there had been no customers today, or yesterday. That the rent was due at the end of the week and they had barely enough to cover it. That the coal was running low and winter was coming. But what good would that do? He would only worry, and worry made him worse.

"The shop is fine," she said. "I finished the pocket watch. The merchant's son will collect it on Friday."

Her father's eyes narrowed. "You fixed it?"

"Yes."

"Clara." He reached for her hand. His fingers were cold and bony. "You shouldn't be doing this work."

"Someone has to."

"You should be married. You should have a husband to take care of you."

Clara looked away. They had this conversation before. Her father meant well, but he didn't understand. She was eighteen years old. She had no dowry. She had no fine clothes or social connections. What man would want her? And even if one did, what would happen to her father? To the shop?

"I don't want a husband," she said. "I want to keep the shop open."

"The shop is dying, Clara."

"Not if I can help it."

Her father shook his head. "You're too stubborn. You get that from your mother."

Clara smiled despite herself. Her mother had died when she was six. She remembered very little, only a warm voice and gentle hands. Her father spoke of her often, especially when Clara frustrated him.

"Rest now," Clara said. She stood and tucked the blanket around him. "I'll bring you some broth later."

"There's no money for broth."

"I'll manage."

She left the room before he could argue. Back downstairs, she returned to the workbench. The pocket watch sat where she had left it, ticking away. She picked up a scrap of paper and wrote out an invoice in her neatest hand. At the bottom, she signed it. C. Wren.

Not Clara Wren. Just C. Wren. If the merchant's son thought her father had done the work, that was fine. If he paid, that was all that mattered.

The bell above the door jingled. Clara looked up, startled. A man stood in the doorway. He was tall and thin, with dark hair and a long coat. He carried a leather case under one arm.

"Good afternoon," Clara said. She wiped her hands on her apron and stepped behind the counter. "Can I help you?"

The man looked around the shop. His gaze took in the empty shelves, the dust on the windowsill, the faded sign above the counter. Clara felt her cheeks flush. The shop must look desperate to someone from outside.

"I'm looking for Mr Wren," the man said. His voice was quiet and well-spoken. Not local.

"My father is unwell," Clara replied. She had said those words so many times now they came easily. "I can help you, or you can leave the item and collect it later."

The man frowned. "I need a repair done quickly. It's urgent."

Clara hesitated. Urgent usually meant expensive. It also meant risky. If she made a mistake, the customer would be angry. But they needed the money. They needed it badly.

"What is it?" she asked.

The man opened his case and pulled out a timepiece. It was beautiful. Gold casing, intricate engravings, a white enamel face. The kind of watch a wealthy man would own. He set it on the counter.

"The mechanism is damaged," he said. "It stopped working yesterday."

Clara picked up the watch carefully. It was heavy in her hand. She opened the case and looked inside. The problem was obvious. One of the gears had broken. It would need replacing.

"I can fix it," she said. "But I'll need a few days."

"I need it by tomorrow."

Clara looked up. "Tomorrow?"

"I'm leaving Birmingham in the morning. The watch is important."

"I can't promise it will be ready by then."

The man studied her for a moment. His eyes were dark and serious. "Are you sure your father can't do it?"

"I'm sure."

"Then I suppose I'll have to trust you." He reached into his pocket and pulled out a coin purse. "How much?"

Clara named a price. It was more than she usually charged, but if the man wanted it done quickly, he could afford to pay. The man didn't blink. He counted out the coins and set them on the counter.

"I'll return tomorrow afternoon," he said. "If it's not ready, I expect a refund."

"It will be ready."

The man nodded and left. The bell jingled again as the door closed behind him. Clara stared at the coins on the counter. It was more money than she had seen in weeks. Enough to pay the rent. Enough to buy coal and food.

She picked up the watch and carried it to the workbench. The broken gear would need replacing. She would have to find one that fit. That meant going through her father's collection of spare parts. It meant working through the night.

But she could do it. She had to.

Clara lit another lamp and pulled the box of spare parts from under the bench. She tipped it out onto the surface. Dozens of tiny gears and springs tumbled across the wood. She sorted through them, holding each one up to the light. Too big. Too small. Wrong shape.

Finally, she found one that looked right. She held it next to the broken gear and nodded. It would work.

The clock on the wall struck five. Outside, the light was fading. Clara could hear the sound of factory workers walking home, their voices carrying through the window. She should go upstairs and check on her father. She should make him something to eat.

Instead, she picked up her tools and began to work.

The hours passed. The shop grew dark except for the circle of light around the workbench. Clara's back ached from bending over the watch. Her eyes burned from staring at the tiny parts. But her hands stayed steady.

She removed the broken gear and cleaned the space where it had been. She fitted the new gear into place and checked the alignment. Perfect. She wound the watch and listened. The ticking started, soft and steady.

Relief flooded through her. She had done it.

She closed the case and set the watch aside. Her hands were shaking now that the work was finished. She rubbed her eyes and looked at the clock. Half past eleven. She had been working for six hours.

Upstairs, she could hear her father coughing again. Guilt twisted in her chest. She had been so focused on the watch that she had forgotten about him. She stood and stretched, her joints cracking.

The coins still sat on the counter. Clara picked them up and counted them. Three shillings and sixpence. She opened the drawer beneath the counter and dropped them inside. They clinked against the few other coins already there. It wasn't much, but it was something.

She wrote out another invoice and signed it. C. Wren. The man would never know who had really fixed his watch. That was for the best.

Clara climbed the stairs to her father's room. He was awake, staring at the ceiling. She brought him water and a slice of bread. It was all they had.

"Did you finish the work?" he asked.

"Yes."

"Good girl." He reached for her hand again. "You're keeping us alive, Clara. I don't know how, but you are."

Clara didn't answer. She sat with him until he fell asleep, then went to her own small room next door. She didn't bother undressing. She lay on top of the blanket and stared at the dark ceiling.

The shop was dying. Her father was dying. And she was the only thing standing between them and ruin.

She thought about the man who had brought in the watch. He had looked at her with doubt, but he had trusted her in the end. That was something. If she could do good work, maybe more customers would come. Maybe word would spread.

Or maybe it wouldn't matter. Maybe the shop would close and they would be thrown out onto the street. Maybe her father would die and she would be left with nothing.

Clara closed her eyes. She was too tired to think about it now. Too tired to worry. She would face tomorrow when it came.

The sound of ticking drifted up from the shop below. Dozens of clocks, all measuring time. All counting down.

She fell asleep to the sound of their rhythm, steady and unchanging, like a hundred small hearts beating in the dark.

Chapter Two

THE OFFICE WAS QUIET except for the ticking. Nathaniel Blackwood sat at his desk and held the pocket watch up to the lamplight. The gold casing gleamed. He opened it and studied the mechanism inside. Every gear sat perfectly in place. The spring tension was exact. The balance wheel turned smoothly, without the slightest wobble.

It was beautiful work. More than beautiful. It was perfect.

Nathaniel closed the watch and set it on the desk. He had collected it from the Wren shop yesterday afternoon. The young woman who ran the counter had handed it to him wrapped in brown paper. She had not met his eyes.

"Your repair is complete, sir," she had said. Her voice was quiet but steady.

"Thank you." Nathaniel had paid her and left. He had not asked questions. Something about the way she held herself told him she did not want to answer any.

Now, alone in his office, he picked up the watch again. He had owned it for three years. It had been a gift from his mother before she died. The mechanism had always been temperamental. Other watchmakers had tried to fix it, but the problem always came back.

This time felt different. The watch ticked with a steady rhythm. No hesitation. No catch. Whoever had repaired it understood not just how watches worked, but how they should work.

C. Wren.

Nathaniel opened the invoice that had come with the watch. The handwriting was neat and small. The signature at the bottom was just a letter and a surname. Nothing more.

He had never heard of C. Wren before. The shop was tucked away on a side street, the kind of place you would walk past without noticing. But the work spoke for itself. This was not the work of an ordinary craftsman. This was the work of someone with real skill.

The door to his office opened. Nathaniel looked up. His factory manager, Mr Simmons, stood in the doorway. He was a broad man with grey whiskers and a permanent frown.

"Morning, Mr. Blackwood," Simmons said. He crossed to the desk without waiting for an invitation. "I see you got your watch back."

"Yes."

"Let me see it then." Simmons held out his hand.

Nathaniel hesitated, then passed the watch over. Simmons turned it over in his thick fingers. He opened the case and squinted at the mechanism.

"Not bad," he said after a moment. "Who did the work?"

"A watchmaker called C. Wren."

Simmons frowned. "Never heard of him."

"Neither had I."

"Well, it is decent work, I suppose. Nothing special though. We have a dozen men here who could do the same." Simmons closed the watch and handed it back. "I wouldn't waste your time tracking him down. Probably just got lucky with this one."

Nathaniel said nothing. He slipped the watch into his waistcoat pocket. Simmons was wrong. This was not luck. This was skill. But there was no point arguing. Simmons dismissed anything that did not come from Blackwood and Sons.

"Anything else?" Nathaniel asked.

"Your father wants to see you. He is in his office."

Nathaniel nodded. Simmons left, closing the door behind him. Nathaniel sat back in his chair and rubbed his eyes. His father always wanted to see him. Usually to complain about something.

He thought about the watch in his pocket. About the small shop with the faded sign. About the young woman who had not met his eyes.

Who was C. Wren?

Nathaniel stood and crossed to the window. His office overlooked the factory floor. Below, rows of workers bent over their benches. The sound of tapping hammers and whirring machines drifted up through the floorboards. Blackwood and Sons produced hundreds of watches every month. They were good watches. Reliable. But they were not special.

Nathaniel had tried to change that. When he returned from Cambridge three years ago, he had been full of ideas. New designs. Better mechanisms. Ways to make watches that would last a lifetime.

His father had rejected every suggestion.

"We make watches that sell," his father had said. "Not watches that sit in museums."

Nathaniel had argued. He had shown his father sketches and calculations. He had explained how small improvements could make a big difference.

His father had listened with cold eyes and then dismissed him.

"You spent three years at Cambridge learning theory," his father had said. "I spent thirty years building this factory. I know what works."

That had been the end of it. Nathaniel had taken his place in the office. He reviewed orders and managed accounts. He attended meetings and signed papers. But he did not design anything. He did not create anything.

He was twenty-six years old and already felt like his life was over.

The memory came back to him then, sharp and painful. Cambridge. The scandal. The reason he had been sent home in disgrace.

He had been in his second year when he discovered the truth. One of his professors had shown him a design for a new type of regulator. It was brilliant. Nathaniel had been excited to show it to his father.

But when he examined it more closely, he realized he had seen it before. The design was almost identical to one his father had used in Blackwood watches five years earlier.

Nathaniel had asked his professor about it. The professor had been confused. He said the design was his own work. He had never shown it to anyone outside the university.

Nathaniel had gone through his father's files. He had found letters. Payments. Proof that his father had been paying university staff for designs. Taking their work and claiming it as his own.

When Nathaniel confronted his father, the old man had not denied it.

"This is how business works," his father had said. "You take what you can and you use it. The weak complain. The strong succeed."

Nathaniel had threatened to go public. His father had threatened to disinherit him. They had fought for weeks. In the end, Nathaniel's older brother Thomas had stepped in.

Thomas had always been the peacemaker. He was four years older than Nathaniel and had worked at the factory since he was eighteen. He understood their father in a way Nathaniel never could.

"Let me handle this," Thomas had said. "I will talk to Father. I will make him see reason."

Nathaniel had agreed. He had returned to Cambridge and tried to focus on his studies. But a month later, Thomas was dead.

The factory collapse. That was what they called it. A section of the factory floor had given way during the night. Thomas had been working late. He had fallen three storeys and died on impact.

The official report said it was an accident. Poor maintenance. Rotten floorboards. No one was to blame.

But Nathaniel had never believed it. Thomas had been investigating something. He had found evidence of more than just stolen designs. He had talked about going to the authorities.

And then he had died.

Nathaniel had come home for the funeral. His father had told him to stay. To take Thomas's place at the factory. Nathaniel had refused. He had wanted to go back to Cambridge. To finish his degree. To get away from Birmingham and the factory and the secrets.

But his father had given him no choice. The scandal at Cambridge had followed him home. Whispers of whistleblowing. Accusations of disloyalty. The university had suggested he take some time away.

So he had stayed. He had taken an office at the factory. He had learned to keep his head down and his mouth shut. He had learned to live with the weight of his brother's death.

Three years later, he was still here. Still trapped.

Nathaniel turned away from the window. He picked up the invoice from his desk and read it again. C. Wren. The handwriting was confident. The signature was simple.

Whoever this person was, they loved their work. Nathaniel could tell from the care that had gone into the repair. Every tiny adjustment had been thought through. Nothing was rushed or careless.

It reminded him of why he had wanted to work with watches in the first place. Not for money or status. But for the craft itself. For the satisfaction of making something perfect.

He wanted to meet C. Wren. He wanted to know who they were. What they thought about design. What they could teach him.

His father would disapprove. Simmons would call it a waste of time. But Nathaniel did not care. For the first time in three years, he felt interested in something.

He sat down at his desk and pulled out a piece of paper. He dipped his pen in the inkwell and began to write.

Dear Mr Wren,

I recently had a timepiece repaired at your establishment. The quality of the work was exceptional. I would like to commission further repairs and possibly discuss a longer arrangement.

Would you be available to meet at your earliest convenience? I am prepared to pay generously for your time and expertise.

Yours sincerely,

Nathaniel Blackwood

He read the letter over twice. It sounded formal. A bit stiff. But that was fine. He did not want to seem too eager.

Nathaniel folded the letter and sealed it with wax. He would have it delivered this afternoon. With luck, C. Wren would reply within a day or two.

He stood and left his office. He had promised to see his father, and putting it off would only make things worse.

The corridor to his father's office was lined with portraits. Past Blackwood men stared down from the walls. His grandfather. His great-grandfather. All of them stern and successful.

Thomas's portrait hung at the end. He looked serious in the painting, but Nathaniel remembered him smiling. Thomas had smiled a lot before he died.

Nathaniel knocked on his father's door.

"Come in," came the reply.

The office was larger than Nathaniel's. It had tall windows that overlooked the street. A heavy desk sat in the centre. Behind it sat Archibald Blackwood.

He was in his sixties but looked younger. His hair was grey but thick. His beard was neatly trimmed. He wore a dark suit with a gold watch chain across his waistcoat. Everything about him spoke of control and power.

"You wanted to see me?" Nathaniel said.

"Sit." His father gestured to the chair across from him.

Nathaniel sat. He kept his face neutral. His father liked to start these meetings with silence. It was a test. To see if Nathaniel would squirm.

Nathaniel had learned not to.

After a moment, his father leaned back in his chair. "Simmons tells me you are chasing after some nobody watchmaker."

"I had a repair done. The work was good."

"And now you want to meet this person?"

"Yes."

"Why?"

"I am curious about their methods."

His father's eyes narrowed. "You are wasting your time. We have plenty of skilled workers here. You do not need to go looking elsewhere."

"I disagree."

"Of course you do." His father picked up a pen and tapped it on the desk. "You always think you know better. Just like your brother."

The mention of Thomas stung. Nathaniel kept his expression blank. "Thomas was right about many things."

"Thomas is dead."

The words hung in the air. Cold and final.

"Yes," Nathaniel said quietly. "He is."

His father set the pen down. "I did not call you here to argue. I called you here to remind you of your responsibilities. You are a Blackwood. You work for Blackwood and Sons. You do not go running after strangers because you are bored."

"I am not bored. I am interested."

"It is the same thing." His father stood and crossed to the window. He looked down at the factory floor, his hands clasped behind his back. "You have always been too idealistic, Nathaniel. You think craft matters more than profit. You think quality is worth the cost. But that is not how the world works."

"Maybe it should be."

His father turned to look at him. For a moment, something flickered in his eyes. Not anger. Something else. Disappointment, maybe.

"Do what you like," his father said finally. "Meet your watchmaker. Waste your time. But do not come crying to me when it leads nowhere."

Nathaniel stood. "Is that all?"

"That is all."

Nathaniel left the office without another word. He walked back down the corridor, past the portraits, past Thomas's face frozen in paint.

He thought about his brother. About the questions Thomas had asked. About the secrets he had uncovered.

Nathaniel had spent three years trying to forget. Trying to keep his head down and survive. But the truth was, he was tired of it. Tired of pretending everything was fine. Tired of working in a factory built on lies.

Maybe meeting C. Wren would not change anything. Maybe it would be just another disappointment.

But maybe it would not.

Back in his office, Nathaniel took out the letter he had written. He called for a messenger and gave him the address. The Wren shop on the side street with the soot-stained windows.

"Deliver this today," Nathaniel said. "Wait for a reply if you can."

The messenger nodded and left.

Nathaniel sat at his desk and pulled out his mother's watch. He held it in his palm and listened to the steady tick. It sounded like a heartbeat. Strong and sure.

Somewhere in Birmingham, C. Wren was working. Maybe in a small shop. Maybe alone. Maybe thinking about gears and springs and all the tiny pieces that made a watch run.

Nathaniel closed his eyes and imagined it. A workbench lit by lamplight. Tools laid out in neat rows. Hands moving with precision and care.

He wanted to be there. He wanted to see it. He wanted to learn.

For the first time in three years, Nathaniel felt some-thing close to hope.

Chapter Three

THE LETTER ARRIVED ON a Tuesday morning. Clara was sweeping the shop floor when she heard footsteps outside. A boy in a messenger's cap pushed open the door. He was about twelve, with a dirty face and nervous eyes.

"Delivery for C. Wren," he said.

Clara set the broom aside and wiped her hands on her apron. "That's me."

The boy held out an envelope. It was made of thick cream paper. The kind expensive people used. Clara's name was written on the front in elegant handwriting.

"Thank you," she said.

The boy touched his cap and left. The bell above the door jingled as it closed.

Clara stood in the empty shop and stared at the envelope. Her hands were trembling. She turned it over. A wax seal held it closed. The seal bore a mark she recognised. A stylised letter B surrounded by decorative flourishes.

Blackwood.

Her stomach dropped. The man who had brought in the watch three days ago. She should have guessed he was someone important. The way he carried himself. The quality of his coat. The gold watch he wore.

She had repaired his timepiece and taken his money. She had thought that would be the end of it. But now he was writing to her. Why?

Clara's first thought was that something had gone wrong. Maybe the watch had stopped working. Maybe he was angry. Maybe he wanted his money back.

She carried the letter to the counter and set it down. Her fingers hovered over the seal. Part of her wanted to throw it away. Pretend it had never arrived. But that would solve nothing.

She broke the seal and unfolded the letter.

The handwriting was the same as on the envelope. Neat and controlled. Clara read it once, then read it again.

Dear Mr. Wren,

I recently had a timepiece repaired at your establishment. The quality of the work was exceptional. I would like to commission further repairs and possibly discuss a longer arrangement.

Would you be available to meet at your earliest convenience? I am prepared to pay generously for your time and expertise.

Yours sincerely,

Nathaniel Blackwood

Clara's hands shook as she set the letter down. Nathaniel Blackwood. She knew that name. Everyone in Birmingham knew the Blackwood family. They owned the largest watch factory in the city. Blackwood and Sons. They made hundreds of watches every month and sold them all over the country.

And now one of them wanted to meet with her.

Clara's mind raced. This was dangerous. If she met with him, he would discover who she really was. He would see that C. Wren was not a man but a young woman. He would realise she had deceived him.

But if she refused, she would lose the chance of more work. More money. The shop needed money desperately. The rent was paid for this month, but next month would come soon enough.

Clara folded the letter and tucked it into her apron pocket. She picked up the broom and continued sweeping. But her thoughts kept returning to the letter. To the elegant handwriting. To the words "prepared to pay generously."

The sound of coughing came from upstairs. Clara set the broom down and hurried up the narrow stairs to her father's room.

He was sitting up in bed, his face pale and drawn. A handkerchief pressed to his mouth. When he lowered it, Clara saw flecks of blood.

"Papa." She crossed to him and took the handkerchief. "Let me get you some water."

"I'm all right." His voice was weak. "Just a cough."

Clara poured water from the jug and held the cup to his lips. He drank a little, then waved it away.

"You should rest," Clara said.

"I've been resting for weeks." He looked at her with tired eyes. "What was that noise downstairs? Did someone come in?"

"Just a delivery boy."

"A customer?"

Clara hesitated. She should tell him about the letter. But she knew what he would say. She knew what his answer would be.

"No," she said. "Just a message."

Her father nodded and lay back against the pillows. "Good. We don't need any trouble."

Clara sat on the edge of the bed. "Papa, what do you know about the Blackwood family?"

Her father's eyes snapped open. "The Blackwoods? Why do you ask?"

"I heard someone mention them. In the street."

Her father's expression darkened. "Stay away from the Blackwoods, Clara. They're powerful people. Dangerous people."

"Dangerous how?"

"They built their fortune on the backs of others. They steal ideas and claim them as their own. They ruin anyone who stands in their way." He reached for her hand. His grip was weak but urgent. "Promise me you'll stay away from them."

"I promise." The lie tasted bitter in her mouth.

Her father relaxed. "Good girl. You're all I have left, Clara. I couldn't bear it if something happened to you."

Clara squeezed his hand. "Nothing will happen to me. I'm careful."

She stayed with him until he fell asleep. Then she went back downstairs. The shop felt too small suddenly. The walls pressed in on her. She needed air. She needed to think.

Clara locked the shop door and walked out into the street. The afternoon was grey and damp. Soot hung in the air like a veil. She pulled her shawl tight around her shoulders and walked.

Her feet carried her through the narrow streets towards the better part of town. Here the buildings were newer. The windows cleaner. The people better dressed.

She stopped outside a dressmaker's shop. Through the window she could see bolts of fabric stacked on shelves. A woman stood at the counter, examining a piece of lace.

Clara pushed open the door. A bell chimed. The woman behind the counter looked up and smiled.

"Clara!" Lizzy Wren set down the lace and hurried around the counter. She was seventeen, a year younger than Clara, with blonde curls and bright blue eyes. "What are you doing here?"

"I needed to talk to someone." Clara glanced at the woman examining the lace. "Are you busy?"

"Mrs. Henderson is just looking." Lizzy lowered her voice. "She's been looking for an hour. I don't think she'll buy anything."

Clara managed a smile. Lizzy had worked at the dressmaker's for two years. She was good at her job. Better than Clara would ever be. Clara had no patience for sewing and stitching. Her skills lay elsewhere.

"Can you take a break?" Clara asked.

"I'll ask Mrs. Shaw." Lizzy disappeared into the back room and returned a moment later with her coat. "She says I can have ten minutes. Come on."

They stepped outside. The street was quieter here.
No factory workers hurrying home. No children playing in the gutters.

"What's wrong?" Lizzy asked. "You look worried."

Clara pulled the letter from her pocket and handed
it to her cousin. Lizzy unfolded it and read. Her eyes
widened.

"Nathaniel Blackwood? Clara, this is wonderful!"

"It's not wonderful. It's dangerous."

"Why?" Lizzy looked at her with confusion. "He
wants to give you more work. That's good, isn't it?"

"He thinks I'm a man."

"Oh." Lizzy's smile faded. "I see the problem."

"If I meet with him, he'll find out the truth. He'll
know I deceived him. He'll tell everyone. The shop will
be ruined."

"Then don't meet with him."

"But we need the money." Clara's voice broke. She
took a breath and steadied herself. "The shop is dying,
Lizzy. We're barely making enough to pay the rent. If
I turn down this work, we might lose everything."

Lizzy folded the letter and handed it back. "Then
you have to take the risk."

"What if he tells people? What if word spreads that a woman is doing watch repairs? No one will trust me. No one will bring me their work."

"Maybe." Lizzy tilted her head. "Or maybe they won't care. You're good at what you do, Clara. Better than most men."

"That doesn't matter. I'm still a woman."

"So?" Lizzy's eyes flashed with defiance. "Why should that stop you? You've been fixing watches for months now. You've done good work. People have been happy with the repairs."

"They don't know it's me doing the work."

"Then maybe it's time they did."

Clara shook her head. "You don't understand. It's not just about the work. It's about what people will think. What they'll say. My father warned me about the Blackwoods. He told me to stay away from them."

"Your father wants to protect you. But he's also afraid." Lizzy's voice softened. "He's been afraid for so long, Clara. Ever since your mother died. Ever since his business started failing. He sees danger everywhere. But you can't live your whole life in fear."

"I'm not afraid."

"Yes, you are." Lizzy reached for her hand. "And that's all right. I'd be afraid too. But you're also brave. You've kept the shop open. You've cared for your father. You've learned a trade that most women would never dare to touch. Don't stop now."

Clara looked down at the letter in her hand. The elegant handwriting. The promise of more work. The danger of discovery.

"What should I do?" she asked quietly.

"Write back to him. But don't agree to meet. Not yet. Tell him you're interested but you need time to consider."

"That's just delaying the decision."

"Maybe." Lizzy smiled. "But it gives you time to think. Time to plan. You don't have to rush into anything."

Clara folded the letter and tucked it back into her pocket. "Thank you, Lizzy."

"That's what family is for." Lizzy hugged her. "Now I have to get back before Mrs. Shaw thinks I've run off. Come and see me again soon. And let me know what you decide."

Clara walked back to the shop alone. The sky was darker now. Rain threatened. She let herself in and locked the door behind her.

The shop was quiet except for the ticking of the clocks. Clara stood behind the counter and looked around. At the empty shelves. At the dusty floor. At the faded sign above the door.

This was her father's legacy. Her grandfather's before him. Three generations of watchmakers. And now it was all falling apart.

She thought about what Lizzy had said. About fear. About bravery. About not living her whole life hiding from the world.

Clara pulled out a sheet of paper and set it on the counter. She picked up her pen and dipped it in ink. Her hand hovered over the page.

She could write a refusal. Polite but firm. Thank him for his interest but explain that she was too busy to take on new commissions.

It would be safe. It would keep her secret. But it would also keep her trapped.

Clara set the pen down. She crumpled the blank paper and threw it away. She pulled out a fresh sheet and began again.

Dear Mr. Blackwood,

Thank you for your kind words regarding the recent repair. I am pleased that the work met your standards.

However, I must respectfully decline your invitation to meet. My current commitments do not allow for additional work at this time.

I wish you well in your endeavours.

Yours sincerely,

C. Wren

Clara read the letter three times. It was polite. Professional. It said everything she needed to say.

She folded it and sealed it with wax. She wrote Nathaniel Blackwood's name on the front. She would send it tomorrow. First thing.

But even as she set it aside, doubt crept in. Was she making the right choice? Was she throwing away an opportunity out of fear?

Clara left the letter on the counter and went upstairs. She looked in on her father. He was sleeping, his breathing shallow and uneven. She pulled the blanket up around his shoulders and touched his forehead. He felt too warm.

In her own small room, Clara lay on the bed and stared at the ceiling. She thought about the letter downstairs. About the words she had written. About the decision she had made.

She thought about Nathaniel Blackwood. About his elegant handwriting and his generous payment. About the watch he had brought her and the skill it had taken to repair it.

She thought about her father's warning. Stay away from the Blackwoods. They're dangerous.

But what if Lizzy was right? What if she was letting fear control her? What if she was passing up a chance to save the shop?

Clara closed her eyes. Her mind drifted. She imagined a different life. One where she didn't have to hide. Where she could work openly as a watchmaker. Where people respected her skill instead of judging her gender.

It was a nice dream. But dreams didn't pay the rent.

She must have fallen asleep because when she opened her eyes again, the room was dark. Clara sat up and rubbed her face. She felt heavy with exhaustion.

Downstairs, the clocks were still ticking. She could hear them through the floorboards. Measuring time. Counting down.

Clara lit a candle and went down to the shop. The letter sat on the counter where she had left it. She picked it up and held it to the candlelight.

Her refusal. Her safe choice. Her coward's choice.

Lizzy's words echoed in her mind. You're brave. Don't stop now.

And beneath that, another voice. Quieter but stronger. Her own voice.

I want to be known for my skill. Not hiding behind initials.

Clara set the letter down. She pulled out a fresh sheet of paper. This time, her hand didn't hesitate.

Dear Mr Blackwood,

Thank you for your letter. I am interested in discussing your proposal.

However, I would prefer to meet at my workshop rather than elsewhere. If this arrangement is acceptable, please send word of a convenient time.

I look forward to hearing from you.

Yours sincerely,

C. Wren

Clara sealed the letter before she could change her mind. She would send it in the morning. She would meet with Nathaniel Blackwood. She would take the risk.

And she would do it on her own terms.

Chapter Four

THE FOG CAME IN thick on Thursday morning. Clara stood at the shop window and watched it roll down the street like smoke. It swallowed the buildings across the way. It turned the gas lamps into dim orange smudges. People appeared and disappeared like ghosts.

Clara pressed her hand against the cold glass. Her breath made a patch of mist. She drew a circle in it with her finger, then wiped it away.

Today was the day. Nathaniel Blackwood would arrive at ten o'clock. She had agreed to meet him. She had told him to come to her workshop.

But she had not told him the truth.

Clara looked down at her clothes. She wore her plainest dress. Grey wool, patched at the elbows. A simple white collar. Her work apron over the top. She had tied her hair back in a tight braid. No ribbons. No decoration.

She looked like a servant. That was the idea.

When Nathaniel arrived, she would tell him she was C. Wren's apprentice. She would say Mr. Wren was too busy to meet but had sent her instead. It was not quite a lie. Just not quite the truth either.

The clock on the wall struck the quarter hour. Nine forty-five. Clara's stomach twisted. She pressed her hand against it and took a deep breath.

She could still change her mind. She could lock the door. Pretend she was not here. Let him knock and get no answer.

But that would solve nothing. She had already agreed to meet. If she backed out now, he might never contact her again. And she needed the work. She needed the money.

Clara turned away from the window. The shop felt too small suddenly. Too exposed. What if he recognised her? What if he remembered her from when he brought in the watch?

No. She had been careful then. She had kept her head down. She had barely spoken. He would not remember.

And if he did? Well, she would deal with that when it happened.

The sound of footsteps outside made her freeze. A shadow appeared in the fog beyond the window. A tall figure. A man.

Clara smoothed down her apron. She clasped her hands together to stop them shaking. The door opened. The bell chimed.

Nathaniel Blackwood stepped into the shop.

He was taller than Clara remembered. His dark coat was buttoned against the cold. His hat dripped with moisture from the fog. He carried a leather case under one arm.

"Good morning," he said. His voice was quiet and polite. "I have an appointment with Mr. Wren."

Clara curtsied. It felt strange. She had never curtsied in her life. But servants did it. Apprentices did it. So she did it too.

"Mr. Wren is occupied with another repair, sir," she said. "He has asked me to assist you in his place."

Nathaniel looked at her properly for the first time. His eyes were dark. Not unkind, but searching. Clara kept her gaze lowered. Servants did not stare at gentlemen.

"I see," Nathaniel said slowly. "And you are?"

"His apprentice, sir."

"Your name?"

Clara hesitated. She should have thought of this. She should have prepared a false name. But her mind had gone blank.

"Clara, sir," she said finally. It was too late to make up something else.

"Clara." Nathaniel nodded. "Well, Clara, I was hoping to speak with Mr. Wren directly. The matter I wish to discuss is rather particular."

"Mr. Wren trusts me to handle most repairs, sir. I can show you what we do here. If you have specific questions, I can pass them along to Mr. Wren."

Nathaniel studied her for a moment longer. Then he set his case on the counter. "Very well. I have brought several pieces that require attention. Perhaps you could examine them and tell me what you think."

Clara moved behind the counter. This was safer. The workbench and tools between them. She could focus on the work instead of the lie.

Nathaniel opened his case and pulled out three watches. He laid them on the counter in a row. "The first two are from my personal collection. The third belongs to a colleague."

Clara picked up the first watch. It was silver with an engraved case. She opened it and looked inside. The mechanism was old but well made. One of the gears had worn down. It would need replacing.

"This one has a damaged gear," she said. "It can be repaired but it will take time to find the right part."

"How much time?"

"A week. Maybe less if I can find something in stock."

Nathaniel nodded. "And the second?"

Clara set the first watch down and picked up the second. This one was gold. More expensive. She opened the case and immediately saw the problem. The mainspring had snapped.

"The mainspring is broken," she said. "I can replace it. Two days."

"Two days?" Nathaniel sounded surprised. "The last watchmaker I spoke to said it would take at least a week."

Clara looked up without thinking. "They were either very busy or very slow. A mainspring replacement is straightforward if you have the parts."

Nathaniel's expression was unreadable. "I see. And do you have the parts?"

"Yes, sir."

"Then two days it is." He gestured to the third watch. "What about this one?"

Clara picked it up. It was cheaper than the other two. Brass casing. Mass produced. The kind Blackwood and Sons made by the hundred. She opened it and examined the mechanism. Nothing was broken. But the timing was off. The balance wheel needed adjusting.

"This just needs regulation," she said. "I can do it now if you like. It will only take a few minutes."

Nathaniel tilted his head slightly. "You can do it while I wait?"

"Yes, sir."

"Then please, go ahead."

Clara carried the watch to her workbench. She could feel Nathaniel watching her. She tried to ignore it. She pulled her stool closer and lit the lamp. The circle of light made everything else fade away.

She picked up her tools. Her hands stopped shaking. This was familiar. This was what she knew.

The balance wheel was easy to access. She made small adjustments to the regulator. Tested it. Adjusted again. Tested again. The watch began to tick more steadily.

"Where did you learn the trade?" Nathaniel's voice came from behind her.

Clara did not look up. "From Mr. Wren, sir."

"He taught you himself?"

"Yes, sir."

"How long have you been working here?"

Clara hesitated. She needed to be vague. Not give too much away. "Several years."

"And before that?"

"I grew up here, sir. In the shop."

That much was true at least.

Nathaniel was silent for a moment. Clara finished the adjustment and closed the watch. She wound it and held it to her ear. The ticking was steady now. She set it on the counter.

"Done," she said.

Nathaniel picked up the watch and examined it. He held it to his ear as Clara had done. A small smile crossed his face.

"Remarkable," he said. "You have skilled hands."

Clara felt her cheeks flush. She looked down at her hands. The ink stains on her fingers. The calluses on her palms. She pulled her sleeves down to cover them.

"Thank you, sir."

Nathaniel set the watch down. He was looking at her hands. Clara realised too late that she had drawn attention to them by trying to hide them.

"Those are not the hands of an ordinary apprentice," Nathaniel said quietly.

Clara's heart hammered. "I do a lot of work, sir."

"Indeed." Nathaniel's tone was thoughtful. Not suspicious exactly, but curious. "Tell me, Clara, what do you think of watch design?"

"Sir?"

"Do you ever think about how watches could be improved? Made more reliable? More accurate?"

Clara looked up at him. This felt like a trap. But she could not help herself. She had thought about these things. Often. Late at night when she could not sleep.

"Sometimes," she admitted.

"And what are your thoughts?"

Clara bit her lip. She should keep quiet. Say something simple. Something an apprentice might say.

But the words came out anyway.

"I think most watches are made too quickly," she said. "Factories focus on quantity over quality. They use cheaper materials. They skip steps. It makes the watches less expensive but also less reliable."

Nathaniel leaned against the counter. "Go on."

"If makers spent more time on each piece, they could create watches that last a lifetime. But that would mean making fewer watches. Charging more money. Most people would not pay for it."

"Would you pay for it?"

"If I could afford it, yes."

"Why?"

Clara looked at the watches on the counter. "Because a watch is not just a tool. It is a promise. It promises to keep time. To be reliable. To be there when you need it. If a watch breaks after a year, it has broken that promise."

Nathaniel was quiet. Clara realised she had said too much. An apprentice would not talk like this. An apprentice would know their place.

"I am sorry, sir," she said quickly. "I spoke out of turn."

"No." Nathaniel's voice was firm. "You spoke with knowledge and passion. Those are rare qualities." He straightened up. "I would like to commission a repair from you. Something more complex than these."

Clara's breath caught. "Sir?"

"I have a pocket watch that belonged to my brother. It has not worked properly in years. Several watchmakers have tried to fix it but none have succeeded." He looked directly at her. "Do you think you could repair it?"

Clara thought about the rent. About her father's medicine. About the empty shelves in the shop. About all the reasons she needed to say yes.

But she also thought about the risk. A complex repair from a Blackwood. If she failed, word would spread. If she succeeded, questions would be asked.

"I would need to see it first, sir," she said carefully. "I cannot promise anything without examining it."

"Of course." Nathaniel reached into his coat and pulled out a pocket watch. It was beautiful. Gold casing with intricate engravings. He handed it to Clara.

She took it carefully. The weight of it felt significant. Not just the metal but the history. This had belonged to his brother. His dead brother.

Clara opened the case. The mechanism inside was complex. More complex than anything she had worked on before. She could see immediately what the problem was. Several gears were misaligned. The escapement was damaged. The mainspring tension was wrong.

It was a challenge. The kind of challenge she loved.

"I can fix this," she said quietly.

"How long will it take?"

"A week. Maybe more."

"And the cost?"

Clara named a price. It was more than she usually charged. But this was complex work. It would take hours. Days, even.

Nathaniel did not blink. "Agreed." He pulled out a purse and counted out coins. More coins than Clara had seen in months. He set them on the counter.

"Half now," he said. "The rest when the work is complete."

Clara stared at the money. It was generous. Too generous. She should feel grateful. Instead she felt uneasy.

"This is more than the repair costs, sir," she said.

"Consider it a deposit on future work. If you repair this watch successfully, I will have more commissions for you. Much more."

Clara picked up the coins slowly. They were cold and heavy in her palm. "Thank you, sir."

"I should be thanking you." Nathaniel picked up his case. "I will return in a week to collect the watch. If you finish sooner, you can send word to my office at Blackwood and Sons."

He moved towards the door. Clara followed him. He paused with his hand on the handle.

"One more thing," he said. "Your apprenticeship. How much longer does it last?"

Clara's mind raced. "I... I am not sure, sir."

"When you complete it, I would like to discuss a position with you. At the factory."

"The factory?" Clara's voice came out higher than she intended.

"We could use someone with your skills. And your insights." Nathaniel smiled slightly. It made him look younger. Less serious. "Think about it."

He opened the door. The fog rolled in, cold and damp. He stepped out into it and disappeared.

Clara stood in the empty shop. Her heart was pounding. Her hands were shaking again. She looked down at the coins in her palm. Then at the pocket watch on the counter. Then at her ink-stained fingers.

He had noticed. He had noticed her hands. Her knowledge. Her passion.

But he had not guessed the truth. He thought she was an apprentice. A talented one perhaps, but still just an apprentice.

Clara closed her fist around the coins. She felt torn between relief and disappointment. She had fooled him. Her disguise had worked.

But part of her had wanted him to see through it. Part of her had wanted him to know who she really was.

Clara shook her head. That was foolish. Dangerous. She could not afford to be discovered. Not yet. Maybe not ever.

She locked the door and carried the coins upstairs. Her father was awake, sitting up in bed. He looked at her with tired eyes.

"Who was that?" he asked. "I heard voices."

"A customer," Clara said. She showed him the coins. "He wants a watch repaired."

Her father's eyes widened. "That's a lot of money."

"It is complex work."

"Who is the customer?"

Clara hesitated. She could not lie to her father. But she could not tell him the whole truth either.

"Someone from Blackwood and Sons," she said finally.

Her father's face darkened. "I told you to stay away from them."

"I know. But we need the money, Papa. You know we do."

"Not from them. Never from them."

"Why?" Clara sat on the edge of the bed. "What happened between you and the Blackwoods?"

Her father looked away. "That is old business. It does not matter now."

"It matters to me."

"All you need to know is that they are not to be trusted. They will use you and then cast you aside." He reached for her hand. "Promise me you will be careful."

"I promise."

"Good girl." He lay back against the pillows. "Now let me rest. I am tired."

Clara kissed his forehead and left the room. She went back downstairs to the workshop. The pocket watch sat on the counter where she had left it. She picked it up and carried it to her workbench.

The fog outside had grown thicker. The world beyond the window had disappeared. Clara felt as though she was alone in the universe. Just her and the watch and the ticking of the clocks.

She opened the watch case and studied the mechanism. It was beautiful work. Whoever had made this had been a master craftsman. But time and damage had taken their toll.

Clara picked up her tools and began to work. Her hands moved with confidence. This was what she was good at. This was what she loved.

As she worked, she thought about Nathaniel Blackwood. About his quiet voice and searching eyes. About the way he had listened when she talked about watches. About the offer he had made.

A position at the factory.

It should have excited her. It should have filled her with hope.

Instead it made her sad. Because she knew she could never accept. She could never walk into that factory as herself. As Clara Wren. She would always have to hide. Always have to pretend.

Unless she was brave enough to tell the truth.

But what would happen then? Would he still want to hire her? Or would he turn away in disgust?

Clara did not know. And she was not sure she wanted to find out.

She bent over the watch and focused on the work. The gears and springs and tiny screws. The precision and patience required. This was real. This was something she could control.

The rest could wait.

Chapter Five

CLARA WORKED LATE INTO the night. The lamp on her workbench cast a small circle of light. Beyond it, the shop was dark. The clocks ticked around her, each one keeping its own rhythm.

She had spent the last three hours examining Nathaniel's pocket watch. It was more complex than anything she had worked on before. The mechanism was intricate. Beautiful. Every gear and spring had been crafted with care.

But it was also damaged. Not just broken. Damaged. As though someone had tried to repair it badly and made things worse.

Clara held a tiny gear up to the light. The teeth were worn on one side. It would need replacing. She set it aside and picked up another piece. This one was bent. She would have to straighten it or find a new one.

She made notes in her workbook. Each problem. Each solution. The list grew longer as the night wore on.

The watch had belonged to Thomas Blackwood. Nathaniel's brother. The one who had died. Clara thought about that as she worked. This watch had stopped when its owner died. Now it sat on her workbench, waiting to tick again.

It felt important. Like bringing something back to life.

Clara set down her tools and rubbed her eyes. The clock on the wall showed half past midnight. She should sleep. But her mind was too busy. Too full of gears and springs and possibilities.

She picked up the coins Nathaniel had given her. They sat in a small pile beside her workbook. More money than she usually earned in a month. Just for the deposit.

Clara counted them again. Then she wrapped them in a cloth and stood. The floorboards creaked as she crossed to the corner of the shop. She knelt down and pried up one of the loose boards. Beneath it was a small space. Dark and dusty.

She had found this hiding place years ago. She used to keep her mother's ring here. The only thing she had left of her. But her father had sold the ring last winter when the coal ran out.

Now the space was empty. Clara placed the cloth inside and replaced the floorboard. She pressed it down until it sat flush with the others. No one would know it was loose unless they looked closely.

She did not like hiding the money. But she could not risk leaving it out. The shop had been broken into twice in the past year. Nothing much had been taken. There was nothing much to take. But thieves were desperate. They would take anything they could sell.

And if her father found the money, he would ask questions. Questions she could not answer.

Clara stood and brushed the dust from her skirt. Her back ached from bending over the workbench. Her fingers were stiff. But she felt satisfied. The watch could be repaired. It would take time. Patience. Skill. But she could do it.

She climbed the stairs to check on her father. His door was open. She could hear him breathing. It sounded rough. Laboured. She stood in the doorway and watched him sleep.

He looked old. Too old. His hair was completely grey now. His face was thin and lined. When had that happened? When had her strong father become this frail man?

Clara tiptoed into the room and pulled the blanket up over his shoulders. He stirred but did not wake. She touched his forehead. It felt warm. Not feverish, but warm.

She went to her own small room and lay down on the bed. She was too tired to undress. She closed her eyes and tried to sleep.

But sleep would not come. Her mind kept turning back to the watch. To Nathaniel. To the way he had looked at her when she talked about watches.

He had listened. Really listened. Not many people did that. Most men dismissed her opinions. Assumed she knew nothing. But Nathaniel had asked questions. He had wanted to know what she thought.

And he had offered her a job. A position at the factory.

Clara rolled onto her side and stared at the dark wall. She should feel excited. Grateful. Instead she felt trapped.

Because she could never take that job. Not as herself. She would always have to hide. Always have to pretend to be someone she was not.

Eventually she drifted into an uneasy sleep.

She woke to the sound of voices. Men's voices. Loud and harsh. Coming from the street below.

Clara sat up and pushed the hair from her face. Grey light filtered through the small window. Morning. She had slept later than usual.

She went to the window and looked down. Two men stood outside the shop. One was Mr. Davies, who ran the butcher's shop three doors down. The other was Mr. Ellis, the baker. They were talking. Gesturing. Looking at her shop.

Clara's stomach tightened. She could not hear what they were saying. But she could guess.

She dressed quickly and went downstairs. The shop was cold. The lamps were out. She had forgotten to bank the fire before going to bed. Now it had died completely.

Clara unlocked the door and stepped outside. The morning air was damp and chill. Mr. Davies and Mr. Ellis stopped talking and looked at her.

"Morning, Miss Wren," Mr. Davies said. He did not smile.

"Good morning." Clara kept her voice steady. "Can I help you?"

"Just passing by," Mr. Ellis said. "Noticed your shop has been quiet lately."

"We're managing."

"Are you?" Mr. Davies crossed his arms. "Because word is you're in debt. Behind on your rent."

Clara's face flushed. "That's not true."

"Isn't it?" Mr. Ellis raised his eyebrows. "I heard your father's been ill. Can't work. And you... well, you're just a girl. What do you know about watches?"

"Enough to keep the shop running."

Mr. Davies snorted. "A girl. Running a watch shop. It's not right. Not natural."

"My father taught me the trade."

"Teaching a daughter is one thing. Letting her run a business is another." Mr. Ellis shook his head. "You should find a husband, Miss Wren. Let a man take care of things."

Clara's hands curled into fists. She wanted to shout at them. Tell them she was as good as any man. Better than most. But she held her tongue.

"Thank you for your concern," she said coldly. "But I can manage."

"Can you?" Mr. Davies leaned closer. "Because I heard you had to pawn your mother's ring just to buy coal. That's not managing. That's failing."

Clara felt as though she had been slapped. How did he know about the ring? Had her father told someone? Or had word just spread?

"Good day, gentlemen," she said. She turned and went back inside. She shut the door firmly behind her.

Her hands were shaking. Her face burned with shame and anger. They had no right. No right to judge her. To gossip about her family.

But they did anyway. Because she was a woman. Because she had dared to do something women were not supposed to do.

Clara leaned against the door and closed her eyes. She took deep breaths until the shaking stopped.

The gossip would spread. It always did. Soon everyone would be talking about the failing watch shop. About the poor girl trying to do a man's work. About how she should give up and find a husband.

She could not let that happen. She could not let them be right.

Clara pushed away from the door. She needed to work. To prove them wrong. To show them she could succeed.

She spent the morning cleaning the shop. Sweeping the floor. Polishing the counter. Washing the windows. It was busy work. Pointless work. But it made her feel better.

At noon, she made soup for her father. Thin soup. Just vegetables and water. But it was hot and it would fill his stomach.

She carried it upstairs. Her father was awake, sitting up in bed. He looked tired. His eyes were sunken and dark.

"Clara." His voice was rough. "What time is it?"

"Noon." She set the bowl on the bedside table. "I made you some soup."

"Thank you." He reached for the spoon but his hand shook. Clara took it from him and fed him herself. Like a child. He did not protest.

When the bowl was empty, he lay back against the pillows. "I heard voices this morning. Who was here?"

"Just some neighbours."

"What did they want?"

Clara hesitated. She did not want to worry him. But she could not lie either.

"They were asking about the shop. About whether we're managing."

Her father's face darkened. "What did you tell them?"

"That we're fine."

"Are we?"

Clara looked away. "We will be."

Her father was quiet for a long moment. Then he said, "You've been working late. I hear you downstairs. In the middle of the night."

"I have a commission. An important one."

"From who?"

Clara's mouth went dry. "A customer."

"What customer?"

"Just... someone who needs a watch repaired."

Her father's eyes narrowed. "You're lying to me."

"I'm not."

"Clara." He reached for her hand. His grip was weak but urgent. "Tell me the truth. Where is this commission from?"

Clara could not meet his eyes. "Blackwood and Sons."

Her father let go of her hand as though she had burned him. "I told you to stay away from them."

"I know. But Papa, we need the money. You know we do."

"Not from them. Never from them."

"Why?" Clara's voice rose. "Why do you hate them so much? What happened?"

Her father's face twisted with pain. Not physical pain. Something deeper. "That is not your concern."

"It is my concern. This is my shop too. My life. I have a right to know."

"No." Her father's voice was hard. Final. "You have no right. You are my daughter. You will do as I say. And I say you will not work for the Blackwoods."

"It's too late. I already took the commission."

"Then give it back."

"I can't. I've already started the work."

Her father tried to sit up but fell back against the pillows. He was breathing hard. His face had gone pale.

"Papa." Clara reached for him but he pushed her away.

"Get out," he said. "Leave me alone."

Clara stood. Tears burned in her eyes. "Papa, please."

"Get out!"

She fled the room. She ran down the stairs and into the shop. The tears came then. Hot and angry. She pressed her hands to her face and tried to stop them.

But they would not stop.

She sank onto her stool and wept. For her father. For the shop. For herself. For the impossible situation she was trapped in.

Eventually the tears stopped. Clara wiped her face with her apron. Her eyes felt swollen. Her head ached.

She looked at the workbench. At the pocket watch lying there. The watch that had caused all this trouble.

She could give it back. Tell Nathaniel she could not do the work. Return his money. Make her father happy.

But then what? They would still be in debt. The shop would still be failing. The gossip would still spread.

And she would have given up. Proven everyone right. Shown that she was just a girl. That she could not manage.

Clara stood and crossed to the window. Outside, the street was busy. People hurried past. Going about their lives. None of them cared about her problems. None of them would help.

She was alone in this.

The afternoon wore on. Clara worked at her bench. She tried to focus on the watch. On the gears and springs. But her mind kept drifting.

At four o'clock, she heard a noise behind her. She turned. Her father stood in the doorway. He was wearing his old coat and his shoes. He looked unsteady on his feet.

"Papa. You should be in bed."

"I need to go out." His voice was hoarse.

"Where?"

"The King's Arms. I need a drink."

Clara's heart sank. The King's Arms was a pub two streets away. Her father went there sometimes. When he had money. When he wanted to forget.

"Papa, you shouldn't drink. Not with your illness."

"My illness is why I need to drink." He moved towards the door. Clara stepped in front of him.

"Please. Just go back to bed. I'll make you some tea."

"I don't want tea. I want gin."

"You don't have any money."

"Then I'll borrow some." He tried to push past her but she held her ground.

"Papa, please."

"Move aside, Clara."

"No."

They stood there for a long moment. Staring at each other. Then her father's shoulders sagged. The fight went out of him.

"Please, Clara," he said quietly. "Just let me go."

Clara stepped aside. What else could she do? She could not stop him. She could not change his mind.

Her father opened the door and walked out into the street. Clara watched him go. He moved slowly. Carefully. Like an old man.

She closed the door and locked it. Then she went back to her workbench and picked up her tools.

The sun was setting when she heard the voices again. Men's voices. Coming from the street. Clara went to the window and looked out.

Her father stood outside the pub down the road. Not the King's Arms, not as reputable. Three men surrounded him. They were laughing. Jeering. One of them pushed him. Her father stumbled but stayed on his feet.

Clara's blood ran cold. She grabbed her shawl and ran outside.

"Leave him alone," she shouted.

The men turned to look at her. They were young. Maybe twenty. Drunk already.

"What's this?" one of them said. "The watchmaker's daughter come to rescue daddy?"

"He's sick. Leave him be."

"He's been telling stories," another man said. "About how he used to be a great watchmaker. How the Blackwoods ruined him. Crying into his gin like a baby."

The men laughed. Clara's father looked at the ground. His face was red with shame.

"Pathetic," the first man said. "Can't even hold his drink. Can't even run his own shop. Has to send his daughter out to do a man's work."

"And what work is that?" the third man leered at Clara. "Bet it's not watch repair. Bet it's something else. Something more... profitable."

Clara's face burned. She knew what he was implying. It made her sick.

"Come on, Papa," she said. She took her father's arm. "Let's go home."

The men stepped aside. Still laughing. Still jeering. Clara helped her father across the street. He was unsteady. He smelled of gin and sweat.

They made it back to the shop. Clara locked the door behind them. Her father sank onto a stool. He put his head in his hands.

"I'm sorry," he said. His voice was muffled. "I'm so sorry, Clara."

"It's all right."

"It's not all right. Nothing is all right." He looked up at her. His eyes were red. "You deserve better than this. Better than me."

"Don't say that."

"It's true. I've failed you. Failed your mother. Failed the shop. Failed everything."

Clara knelt beside him. "You haven't failed. You're just sick. When you get better, things will improve."

Her father shook his head. "I'm not going to get better, Clara. We both know that."

"Don't talk like that."

"It's the truth. I'm dying. Slowly. And when I'm gone, you'll be alone. With nothing. No shop. No money. No future."

"That's not true. I'll keep the shop going. I'll make it work."

"How?" Her father's voice was bitter. "You're a woman. No one will take you seriously. No one will trust you. You'll fail just like I did."

"I won't fail." Clara's voice was fierce. "I'll succeed. I'll prove them all wrong. I'll make this shop the best watch repair shop in Birmingham."

Her father looked at her. Really looked at her. For the first time in weeks, she saw something other than defeat in his eyes. She saw pride.

"You're your mother's daughter," he said quietly. "Stubborn. Strong. She would be proud of you."

Tears stung Clara's eyes. "Then let me do this. Let me work on this commission. Let me save the shop."

Her father was silent for a long time. Then he nodded. "All right. But be careful. The Blackwoods are dangerous. Don't trust them."

"I won't."

"And Clara?" He took her hand. "Whatever happens, know that I love you. And I'm proud of you. Even if I don't say it enough."

"I know, Papa."

Clara helped her father upstairs and into bed. She stayed with him until he fell asleep. Then she went back down to the shop.

She sat at her workbench and looked at the pocket watch. At all the broken pieces. At all the work still to be done.

But she felt different now. Stronger. More determined.

Let them gossip. Let them mock. Let them say she would fail.

She would prove them all wrong.

Clara picked up her tools and began to work.

Chapter Six

NATHANIEL SAT AT HIS desk and stared at the papers in front of him. Production numbers. Orders. Costs. The same reports he reviewed every week. The same columns of figures that meant nothing to him.

He set down his pen and rubbed his eyes. A week had passed since he had left the pocket watch with Clara. A week of wondering if she could repair it. If she would succeed where others had failed.

The door to his office opened without a knock. Nathaniel looked up. Basil Thorn stood in the doorway.

Basil was broad-shouldered and well-dressed. Too well-dressed for a foreman. His dark hair was slicked back with oil. His sharp eyes took in everything. He smiled, but the smile never reached his eyes.

"Good morning, Mr Blackwood." Basil walked into the office and closed the door behind him. "I hope I'm not disturbing you."

"What do you want, Basil?"

"Just checking in." Basil leaned against the desk. Too casual. Too familiar. "I heard an interesting rumour this morning."

"I don't care for rumours."

"This one might interest you." Basil picked up a paperweight from the desk and turned it over in his hands. "Word is you've been seeking out mystery artisans. Small workshops. Independent craftsmen."

Nathaniel kept his face neutral. "I'm always looking for skilled workers."

"Are you?" Basil set the paperweight down. "Because it seems odd. We have plenty of skilled workers here. The best in Birmingham, some say. Yet you go looking elsewhere."

"I like to know what's available."

"Or perhaps you're looking for something specific. Something we don't have here." Basil's smile widened. "Someone with particular talents."

"Get to the point, Basil."

"The point is that people talk. They wonder why the son of Archibald Blackwood needs to go outside the family business. They wonder if perhaps you're dissatisfied with what we produce here."

"What I do is my own concern."

"Is it?" Basil straightened up. "Because your father might see it differently. He might think you're undermining the family name. Going behind his back."

Nathaniel stood. He was taller than Basil but Basil was broader. Stronger. "Are you threatening me?"

"Not at all." Basil held up his hands. "Just offering friendly advice. Be careful who you do business with. Small workshops. Unknown artisans. They can't always be trusted. And if word gets out that you prefer their work to ours, well..." He shrugged. "It wouldn't look good."

"Thank you for your concern." Nathaniel's voice was cold. "Now if you'll excuse me, I have work to do."

Basil moved towards the door. He paused with his hand on the handle. "One more thing. This mystery artisan of yours. Does your father know about them?"

"That's none of your business."

"I'll take that as a no." Basil opened the door. "Just remember what I said. Be careful. Secrets have a way of coming out. And when they do, people get hurt."

He left, closing the door softly behind him.

Nathaniel sat back down. His jaw was tight. His hands clenched into fists.

Basil Thorn. The man was a snake. Always watching. Always waiting for an opportunity to advance himself. He had been angling for a promotion for months. He wanted Nathaniel's position. Maybe even his father's position.

And he would do anything to get it.

Nathaniel forced himself to breathe slowly. To calm down. Getting angry would solve nothing.

He looked at the clock on the wall. Half past ten. Clara should be finishing the repair soon. If she succeeded. If the watch worked.

Nathaniel picked up his pen and tried to focus on the papers. But his mind kept drifting. To the watch.

To Clara. To her ink-stained fingers and intelligent eyes.

The morning dragged on. Nathaniel signed papers. Reviewed reports. Attended a meeting with his father and several factory managers. Basil was there, of course. Smiling his cold smile. Making suggestions. Always careful to seem helpful while undermining Nathaniel at every turn.

When the meeting finally ended, Nathaniel returned to his office. He was exhausted. Frustrated. He wanted to leave. To walk. To clear his head.

A knock at the door made him look up.

"Come in."

The door opened. A young clerk stood there. "Sorry to disturb you, Mr Blackwood. There's someone here to see you. A Miss Clara. She says you're expecting her."

Nathaniel's heart jumped. "Send her in."

The clerk disappeared. A moment later, Clara entered the office.

She looked nervous. She wore the same plain grey dress she had worn before. Her hair was pulled back in a simple braid. She carried a small wrapped package.

"Good afternoon," she said quietly.

"Clara." Nathaniel stood. "Please, come in. Close the door."

She did as he asked. She stood in front of his desk, holding the package with both hands.

"Is that the watch?" Nathaniel asked.

"Yes, sir."

"May I see it?"

Clara set the package on the desk and unwrapped it carefully. The pocket watch lay inside, gleaming in the afternoon light.

Nathaniel picked it up. His hands were not quite steady. This watch had belonged to Thomas. His brother. His friend. The last link to someone he had lost.

He opened the case. The mechanism inside looked perfect. Every gear in place. Every spring aligned. He held it to his ear.

Tick. Tick. Tick.

The sound was steady. Strong. The watch was alive again.

Nathaniel closed his eyes. For a moment he could almost see Thomas. Hear his voice. Feel his presence.

"Sir?" Clara's voice was soft. Concerned. "Is something wrong?"

Nathaniel opened his eyes. "No. Nothing is wrong." He looked at her. Really looked at her. "This is perfect. Better than perfect. You've done something no one else could do."

Clara's face flushed. "It was complex work. But the watch was well made to begin with. It just needed patience."

"And skill."

"Perhaps."

Nathaniel set the watch on the desk. He pulled out his purse and counted out coins. The remainder of the payment. Plus more.

"This is too much, sir," Clara said.

"It's what you deserve."

"But we agreed on a price."

"And I'm choosing to pay more." Nathaniel pushed the coins across the desk. "You've given me something precious. Something I thought was lost forever. That's worth more than money."

Clara hesitated. Then she took the coins and put them in her pocket. "Thank you, sir."

"I have another question for you." Nathaniel sat on the edge of the desk. "How would you like more work?"

Clara looked uncertain. "What kind of work?"

"I meant what I said before. About a position here. At the factory." Nathaniel gestured around the office. "We have skilled workers. But we could use someone with your talents. Someone who understands the finer points of watch repair."

"I'm not sure I'd be suitable, sir."

"Why not?"

"I'm just an apprentice. I don't have experience in a factory setting."

"You have skill. That's more important." Nathaniel leaned forward. "I can't offer you a permanent position immediately. My father would need convincing. But I could bring you in temporarily. As a consultant. You could work on special projects. Repairs that need particular attention."

Clara bit her lip. "I would need to think about it."

"Of course. Take your time." Nathaniel pulled out a card and wrote on the back of it. "Here. This is my private address. If you decide you're interested, send word. We can arrange the details."

Clara took the card and looked at it. Then she looked up at him. "May I ask you something, sir?"

"Please."

"Why are you doing this? Why do you want to help me?"

Nathaniel thought about the question. About all the reasons. About his boredom with the factory. His frustration with his father. His desire to find something real. Something meaningful.

But he said simply, "Because you're talented. And talent should not be wasted."

Clara nodded slowly. "Thank you, sir. I'll think about your offer."

"Good." Nathaniel stood. "Was there anything else?"

"No, sir."

"Then I won't keep you."

Clara curtsied and turned towards the door. She had just reached it when it opened suddenly.

Basil Thorn stood in the doorway. He looked at Clara. Then at Nathaniel. His eyes narrowed.

"Sorry to interrupt," Basil said. His voice was smooth. Dangerous. "I didn't realise you had a visitor."

"This is Clara," Nathaniel said. "She's just delivered a repair."

"A repair." Basil stepped aside to let Clara pass. But his eyes followed her. Sharp. Suspicious. "I see."

Clara hurried past him and disappeared down the corridor.

Basil watched her go. Then he turned back to Nathaniel. "That's your mystery artisan? That girl?"

"She's an apprentice from a local shop."

"Is she?" Basil walked into the office. "Interesting. What shop?"

"That's confidential."

"Of course." Basil smiled. "She seems very young. Very... modest. Not the sort you'd expect to be doing high-quality repair work."

"Appearances can be deceiving."

"They certainly can." Basil picked up the pocket watch from the desk. "Is this what she repaired? Your brother's watch?"

Nathaniel's jaw tightened. "Put that down."

"I'm just looking." Basil turned the watch over in his hands. "Nice work. Very nice. Almost too good for a simple apprentice."

"Basil."

"I wonder what her master is like. This Mr... or M iss... what was the name again?"

"I said that's confidential."

"Right. Confidential." Basil set the watch down. "You know what I think? I think there's more to this story than you're telling me."

"I don't care what you think."

"You should." Basil's smile faded. "Because I'm not the only one who'll be curious. Other people will wonder. Other people will ask questions."

"Let them ask."

"And what will you tell them? That you're hiring mysterious young women to do special work? That you prefer their skills to those of your own employees?" Basil shook his head. "That won't sit well with your father. Or with the board."

"Are you finished?"

"Almost." Basil moved towards the door. "Just remember what I said. Secrets bring scandal. And scandal destroys reputations. Yours. Hers. Everyone involved."

He left before Nathaniel could respond.

Nathaniel stood alone in his office. His hands were shaking with anger. Or was it fear?

Basil was right about one thing. This was dangerous. If word got out about Clara, she would be destroyed. Her reputation. Her livelihood. Everything.

And it would be Nathaniel's fault.

He picked up the pocket watch and held it. The ticking was steady. Reliable. A promise kept.

But what promises had he made to Clara? And what promises could he keep?

Nathaniel sat down at his desk. He pulled out a piece of paper and began to write.

Dear Clara,

I want to clarify my earlier offer. The position I mentioned would be discreet. You would work in a private workshop, away from the main factory floor. No one would need to know your identity or your background.

I understand this is unusual. I understand you may have concerns. But I believe your talent deserves recognition. And I would like to help you achieve that.

If you're interested, we can discuss the details further. But only if you're comfortable. I will not press you.

The offer stands. Take as long as you need to decide.

Yours sincerely,

Nathaniel Blackwood

He read the letter twice. Then he sealed it and called for a messenger.

"Deliver this to the Wren watch shop," he said. "Wait for a reply if there is one."

The messenger left. Nathaniel sat back in his chair.

He had made his offer. Now it was up to Clara.

But in the back of his mind, he could hear Basil's voice. Warning him. Threatening him.

Secrets bring scandal.

Nathaniel looked at the pocket watch on his desk. It ticked steadily. Counting down the seconds.

How long before everything fell apart?

Clara walked quickly through the factory corridors. Her heart was racing. Her hands clutched the coins in her pocket.

She could hear footsteps behind her. Heavy footsteps. Someone following.

She glanced back. Basil Thorn was there. Not close. But watching. His sharp eyes followed her every move.

Clara quickened her pace. She reached the main entrance and pushed through the doors. Outside, the air was cold and damp. Smoke hung over the city like a blanket.

She did not stop walking until she was three streets away from the factory. Only then did she allow herself to slow down.

Her hands were still shaking. Not from cold. From something else. Fear. Excitement. She was not sure which.

The meeting with Nathaniel had gone well. Better than well. He had been pleased with the repair. More than pleased. And he had offered her more work.

A position at the factory. Secret. Discreet. A chance to prove herself.

But there was a problem. Basil Thorn.

The way he had looked at her. Like a cat watching a mouse. Suspicious. Calculating. Dangerous.

He knew something was not right. And he would not stop until he found out what.

Clara reached her shop and let herself in. The familiar smell of oil and metal greeted her. The ticking of the clocks surrounded her.

She should feel safe here. But she did not.

She had stepped into something larger than herself. Larger than her small shop and her secret work.

She had stepped into the world of the Blackwoods. And there were people there who would not welcome her. People who would see her as a threat.

Clara locked the door and leaned against it. She pulled out the coins from her pocket and counted them.

Enough to pay two months' rent. Enough to buy medicine for her father. Enough to keep them going.

But at what cost?

Clara climbed the stairs to check on her father. He was sleeping. She stood in the doorway and watched him breathe.

She had to protect him. Protect the shop. Protect everything they had left.

But she also had to move forward. To take risks. To prove she could do this.

Clara went to her own room and pulled out Nathaniel's card. She read the address on the back. Then she tucked it under her pillow.

She would think about his offer. Carefully. Seriously.

Because this might be her only chance. Her only opportunity to be something more than a secret. More than a girl hiding behind initials.

But she would have to be careful. Very careful.

Because Basil Thorn was watching. And he would not stop until he uncovered the truth.

Chapter Seven

CLARA STOOD OUTSIDE THE factory gates and looked up at the building. It was enormous. Four storeys of dark brick and tall windows. Smoke poured from chimneys on the roof. The sign above the entrance read Blackwood and Sons in gold letters.

She had walked past this factory dozens of times. But she had never been inside.

Now she was about to enter. Not as a visitor. As a worker.

Clara pulled her shawl tighter and walked through the gates. A guard stood in a small wooden hut. He looked at her with disinterest.

"Name?"

"Clara." She had decided not to use her surname. The less people knew about her, the better.

"You're expected. Through the main doors. Ask for Mr Simmons."

Clara nodded and walked towards the entrance. Her heart was hammering. Her hands felt cold despite the warmth of the day.

She had sent word to Nathaniel three days ago. Accepting his offer. Agreeing to work in the factory. She had told her father she was helping a customer with inventory. He had not questioned her. He was too weak to ask many questions anymore.

The main doors were heavy. Clara pushed them open and stepped inside. The noise hit her first. A roar of machinery. Hammering. Grinding. The sound of a hundred workers all doing their jobs at once.

Then came the smell. Oil. Metal. Sweat. It was thick in the air. It caught in her throat.

Clara stood in the entrance hall and tried not to panic. A man approached her. He was broad and grey-haired with a permanent frown.

"You Clara?"

"Yes, sir."

"I'm Simmons. Factory manager. Mr Blackwood said you'd be starting today." He looked her up and down. His expression was not welcoming. "Follow me."

Clara followed him down a corridor. The noise grew louder. They passed rooms full of workers bent over benches. Women and men. Some young. Some old. All focused on their tasks.

Simmons stopped at a door. He opened it and gestured for Clara to enter. Inside was a small room. Bare brick walls. A single window covered with grime. A wooden bench along one wall. Shelves stacked with boxes and parts.

"This will be your workspace," Simmons said. "You'll work alone. No talking to the other workers. No wandering the factory. You do your work and you leave. Understood?"

"Yes, sir."

"Good." He pulled a grey dress from a hook on the wall. "This is your uniform. Put it on. There's a screen in the corner."

Clara took the dress. It was rough cotton. Plain. Worn. She went behind the screen and changed. The dress was too big. It hung loose on her small frame. But it would do.

When she emerged, Simmons was still waiting. He looked at her critically. "You'll need to tie your hair back properly. Can't have it getting caught in machinery."

Clara pulled her braid tighter and secured it with pins.

"That's better." Simmons walked to the shelves and pulled down a wooden box. He set it on the bench. "These are old mechanisms. Damaged. Discarded. Mr Blackwood wants you to see if any can be salvaged. Repaired. Made useful again."

Clara looked at the box. It was full of watch parts. Gears. Springs. Broken cases. All jumbled together.

"How long do I have?"

"As long as it takes. But don't waste time. We pay by results here. Not by the hour." Simmons moved towards the door. "Someone will check on you later. Stay here. Don't cause trouble."

He left. The door closed behind him.

Clara stood alone in the small room. The noise from the factory filtered through the walls. A constant roar. Like being inside the belly of a beast.

She sat on the bench and opened the box. The parts inside were dirty. Covered in dust and oil. She began to sort through them. Separating the usable from the hopeless.

It was familiar work. Calming. She lost herself in it.

Time passed. Clara had no idea how much. There was no clock in the room. The light from the window barely changed. She worked steadily. Examining each piece. Setting aside those that could be saved.

The door opened suddenly. Clara looked up. An old man stood in the doorway. He was thin and stooped. His hair was white. His face was lined with wrinkles. But his eyes were sharp and kind.

"Hello there," he said. His voice was gentle. "You must be the new girl."

"Yes, sir."

"No need for sir. I'm just Pell. Mr. Pell if you want to be formal." He shuffled into the room and peered at the parts spread across the bench. "What have you got here then?"

"Old mechanisms. I'm sorting through them."

"Are you now?" Mr. Pell picked up a gear and held it to the light. "Hmm. This one's worn. But the teeth are still good. You could use it if you filed down the rough edges."

Clara looked at the gear. He was right. "I was thinking the same thing."

Mr. Pell smiled. "Were you? Good eye. Not many would see that." He set the gear down and looked at her properly. "What's your name then?"

"Clara."

"Clara. Nice name. How long have you been working with watches?"

Clara hesitated. She did not want to give too much away. "A few years."

"A few years." Mr. Pell nodded. "And who taught you?"

"My father."

"Your father. He must be a good teacher. You've got skilled hands." He gestured to the bench. "May I?"

Clara moved aside. Mr. Pell sat down and began examining the parts she had sorted. He picked them up one by one. Studied them. Set them down again.

"You've got a good eye," he said finally. "Better than most of the lads we have here. They rush. Make mistakes. But you take your time. That's the mark of a real craftsman."

"Thank you."

"Don't thank me. I'm just stating facts." Mr. Pell stood slowly. His knees creaked. "I'm supposed to be supervising you. Making sure you know what you're doing. But I can see you don't need much supervising."

"I'll work hard."

"I'm sure you will." Mr. Pell moved towards the door. "If you need anything, my workshop is two doors down. Just knock. I'm always happy to help."

"Thank you, Mr. Pell."

He left. Clara felt lighter somehow. Mr. Pell seemed kind. Genuine. Not like Simmons with his cold eyes and harsh words.

She went back to work. The pile of usable parts grew slowly. Some just needed cleaning. Others required more work. Straightening. Filing. Adjusting.

Clara picked up a broken mechanism. The escapement was damaged. But the balance wheel was intact. She could salvage it.

She was examining it closely when the door opened again. This time she did not look up immediately. She assumed it was Mr. Pell returning.

"I see you're settling in."

Clara's head snapped up. Nathaniel stood in the doorway. He looked tired. His jacket was unbuttoned. His hair slightly mussed.

"Mr. Blackwood." Clara stood quickly.

"Please. Don't get up." Nathaniel closed the door behind him. "I wanted to see how you were managing."

"Well enough, sir."

Nathaniel walked to the bench and looked at the parts she had sorted. His expression was thoughtful. "You've made good progress."

"Mr. Pell helped. He gave me some advice."

"Pell is one of our best." Nathaniel picked up the mechanism Clara had been examining. "What do you think of this one?"

"The escapement is damaged. But the balance wheel is good. If I can find a replacement escapement, I can repair it."

"We have spare parts. I'll have someone bring you a box." Nathaniel set the mechanism down. "How are you finding the factory?"

Clara chose her words carefully. "It's very different from what I'm used to."

"I imagine it is." Nathaniel leaned against the wall. "Is the noise bothering you?"

"A little. But I'm getting used to it."

"Good." He was quiet for a moment. Then he said, "I want you to know that you're safe here. This room is private. No one will disturb you except Pell and myself. And Simmons, occasionally. But I've told him to leave you alone as much as possible."

"Thank you."

"You don't need to thank me. You're doing me a favour. These parts have been sitting unused for months. If you can salvage even half of them, it will save us money."

Clara nodded. She wanted to believe him. But she could not shake the feeling that this was dangerous. That someone would discover who she really was.

"Mr. Blackwood," she said quietly. "What if someone asks questions? About who I am? Where I came from?"

"They won't. You're just another worker. There are dozens of people in this factory. No one pays attention to new faces." Nathaniel straightened up. "But if anyone does ask, you're a temporary worker. Hired for a specific job. That's all they need to know."

"And your father? Does he know I'm here?"

Nathaniel's expression hardened. "No. And he won't. I've made sure of that."

Clara felt a chill. "What about Mr. Thorn? He saw me. He knows something isn't right."

"Basil is suspicious by nature. But he has no proof of anything. And as long as you stay in this room and keep your head down, he won't find any." Nathaniel moved towards the door. "I should go. I don't want anyone wondering why I'm spending so much time here."

"Of course."

He paused with his hand on the door handle. "Clara?"

"Yes?"

"You're doing good work. Better than I expected. Keep it up."

He left before she could respond.

Clara sat back down at the bench. Her hands were shaking slightly. The conversation had unsettled her.

Nathaniel was trying to protect her. But what if he could not? What if Basil discovered the truth? What if his father found out?

Clara pushed the thoughts away. She had made her choice. She was here. She would do the work. And she would prove that she belonged.

The afternoon wore on. Clara worked steadily. The pile of salvaged parts grew. She lost track of time again. The noise of the factory became background. Almost comforting in its constancy.

The door opened. Clara looked up, expecting Mr. Pell or Nathaniel.

Instead, three young men stood in the doorway. They were rough-looking. Dirty clothes. Hard eyes. They stared at her with undisguised curiosity.

"Well, well," one of them said. He was tall with a crooked nose. "What have we here?"

"A girl," another said. He was shorter. Stockier. "What's a girl doing in here?"

"Working," Clara said. She kept her voice steady. "Same as you."

"Same as us?" The tall one laughed. "I don't think so. We do real work. Factory work. What do you do? Sew buttons?"

"I repair watches."

The three men exchanged glances. Then they laughed. It was a harsh sound. Mocking.

"Repair watches?" The short one shook his head. "You? A little girl?"

"I know what I'm doing."

"Do you?" The tall one stepped into the room. "Show us then. Prove it."

Clara did not move. She kept her eyes on them. Watching. Waiting.

"Go on," the third man said. He had not spoken before. His voice was quieter. But no less threatening. "Show us how clever you are."

"I have work to do. Please leave."

"Please leave," the tall one mimicked. "Did you hear that? She's got manners. Thinks she's better than us."

"I don't think that."

"Yes, you do. I can see it in your face. You think because you're working for Mr. Blackwood, you're special. But you're not. You're just a girl playing at being a watchmaker."

Clara stood. She was small. Much smaller than any of them. But she would not be intimidated.

"I said I have work to do. Now leave."

The tall one moved closer. Too close. Clara could smell the sweat on him. The tobacco on his breath.

"Make me," he said.

The door opened again. Mr. Pell stood there. His expression was stern.

"What's going on here?" he demanded.

The three men stepped back. The tall one shrugged. "Nothing. Just introducing ourselves to the new girl."

"Get back to work. All of you."

"We were just leaving." The tall one winked at Clara. "See you around."

The three men left. Mr. Pell watched them go. Then he turned to Clara.

"Are you all right?"

"Yes. Thank you."

"Those lads are troublemakers. Always have been."
Mr. Pell came into the room and closed the door.
"Don't let them bother you. They're all talk."

"I wasn't bothered."

Mr. Pell smiled. "No. I don't suppose you were.
You've got a strong spirit. That's good. You'll need it
here."

Clara sat back down. Her heart was still racing. But
she would not show it.

Mr. Pell lingered. "Can I give you some advice?"

"Please."

"Keep to yourself. Don't engage with the other
workers. Don't give them reasons to notice you." He
paused. "I don't know why Mr. Blackwood brought
you here. But I know it's unusual. And unusual things
attract attention. The less attention you attract, the
safer you'll be."

"I understand."

"Good." Mr. Pell moved towards the door. "I'll
check on you again later."

When he left, Clara sat in silence. The words of the
three men echoed in her mind. You're just a girl playing
at being a watchmaker.

But she was not playing. She was a watchmaker. A good one. And she would prove it.

Clara picked up a broken mechanism. One that everyone else had discarded as hopeless. She examined it carefully. The damage was extensive. But not impossible to fix.

She spent the next hour working on it. Cleaning. Adjusting. Replacing parts. Her hands moved with precision. With confidence.

Finally, she wound it. Held it to her ear.

Tick. Tick. Tick.

The mechanism worked. She had brought it back to life.

Clara set it on the bench and looked at it. Pride swelled in her chest. She had done this. No one else. Just her.

The door opened one more time. Nathaniel stood there. He looked at the bench. At the repaired mechanism. At Clara.

"You fixed it," he said quietly.

"Yes."

"How many said it was impossible?"

"I don't know. But someone must have. Otherwise it wouldn't have been discarded."

Nathaniel walked to the bench and picked up the mechanism. He held it. Listened to it tick. A smile crossed his face.

"This is remarkable," he said. "No one else could do this. I've watched a dozen men try. They all failed."

"Maybe they didn't try hard enough."

"Or maybe they didn't have your skill." Nathaniel set the mechanism down. He looked at her with something in his eyes. Admiration. Respect. Something more.

"Thank you," Clara said quietly.

"For what?"

"For giving me this chance. For believing I could do it."

"I should be thanking you. You've proven me right." Nathaniel hesitated. Then he said, "I want you to know something. What you're doing here matters. It's important. Not just for the factory. But for you. For all the women who come after you."

Clara did not know what to say. The words moved her. Frightened her. Inspired her.

"I'll do my best," she said finally.

"I know you will."

Nathaniel left. Clara sat alone in the small room. The noise of the factory surrounded her. But she felt different now.

She felt proud. And terrified. Because she had proven herself today. She had shown what she could do.

But she had also been seen. Noticed. Questioned.

And somewhere in this factory, people were watching. Wondering. Asking questions she could not answer.

Clara looked at the repaired mechanism. At the proof of her skill.

She would keep working. Keep proving herself. But she would also have to be careful.

Very careful.

Because one mistake could destroy everything.

Chapter Eight

CLARA HAD BEEN WORKING at the factory for two weeks when Nathaniel brought the new watches to her room.

She heard his footsteps in the corridor. Two knocks on the door. Then he entered, carrying a wooden case.

"Good morning," he said.

"Good morning, Mr. Blackwood."

Nathaniel set the case on the bench. "I have something I'd like your opinion on."

Clara stood and wiped her hands on her apron. Nathaniel opened the case. Inside were six pocket watches. They looked identical. Silver cases with simple engravings. Standard Blackwood and Sons designs.

"We're launching a new line," Nathaniel said. "These are the prototypes. I wanted someone to examine them before we begin production."

"Why me?"

"Because you see things others don't." Nathaniel picked up one of the watches and handed it to her. "Tell me what you think."

Clara took the watch carefully. She opened the case and looked at the mechanism inside. It was well made. Clean. Efficient. Exactly what she would expect from a factory production.

But there was nothing special about it.

"It's good work," Clara said slowly.

"But?"

Clara looked up at him. "You want me to be honest?"

"Always."

"It's boring."

Nathaniel smiled. Not offended. Interested. "Go on."

"It's reliable. It will keep time. It will sell." Clara set the watch down. "But there's no care in it. No thought. It's made to be functional. Not beautiful."

"Most people just want functional."

"Maybe. But wouldn't it be better to give them something more?" Clara picked up the watch again. "Look at this escapement. It works. But it could be more elegant. The design is clunky. If you changed the angle here..." She gestured with her finger. "...and reduced the weight here... the watch would be more accurate. And it would look better too."

Nathaniel leaned closer. "Show me."

Clara took a pencil from her bench and a scrap of paper. She sketched quickly. A modified escapement. Simpler. More graceful.

Nathaniel studied the drawing. His expression was thoughtful. "This would work?"

"Yes. It's a small change. But it makes a difference."

"Would it cost more to produce?"

"Maybe a little. But not much." Clara set the pencil down. "The problem is time. This design takes more skill. More attention. Most factory workers wouldn't bother. They'd rush through it."

"But you wouldn't."

"No."

Nathaniel was quiet for a moment. Then he said, "What if I told you this line was meant to be special? Better than our usual production. Something to show what Blackwood and Sons can do when we take our time."

"Then I'd say you need to rethink the entire design."

Nathaniel laughed. It was a warm sound. Genuine. "You don't hold back, do you?"

"You asked for honesty."

"I did." Nathaniel pulled out a stool and sat down. "All right. If you were designing this watch, what would you change?"

Clara hesitated. This felt dangerous. Presumptuous. She was just a temporary worker. A girl hiding in a back room. Who was she to tell Nathaniel Blackwood how to design watches?

But he was asking. And he seemed to truly want to know.

"Everything," Clara said finally.

"Everything?"

"The case is fine. Simple. Classic. But the mechanism could be better. More refined." Clara picked up
another watch from the case. "And the balance wheel.
It's functional but not precise. If you used better materials, adjusted the weight distribution, you could improve accuracy by several seconds per day."

Nathaniel leaned forward. "How would you do
that?"

Clara found herself explaining. Showing him. Using
the watches from the case as examples. Pointing out
flaws. Suggesting improvements.

Nathaniel listened. He asked questions. Good
questions. Questions that showed he understood
what she was talking about.

"You studied mechanical arts at Cambridge," Clara
said. "Didn't they teach you this?"

"They taught me theory. Not practice." Nathaniel
picked up the watch Clara had been holding. "My
professors cared more about principles than craftsmanship. They wanted to understand how watches
worked. Not how to make them better."

"That seems backwards."

"It is." Nathaniel set the watch down. "My brother used to say the same thing."

Clara's heart skipped. "Your brother?"

"Thomas. He was older than me by four years." Nathaniel's voice changed. Became quieter. Sadder. "He died three years ago."

"I'm sorry."

"Thank you." Nathaniel was silent for a moment. Then he said, "Thomas loved watches. Not the business side. Not the factory. Just the craft. He used to spend hours taking them apart and putting them back together. Trying to understand how they worked."

Clara's hands felt cold. She remembered her father's warnings. Stay away from the Blackwoods. They're dangerous.

But she also remembered something else. A young man who used to come to the shop. Years ago. Before her father got sick. Before everything fell apart.

He had been kind. Curious. He had asked her father questions about watch repair. He had been learning the trade.

Could that have been Thomas?

"Where did he learn?" Clara asked carefully. "About watches?"

"From a small watchmaker in Birmingham. I don't remember the name." Nathaniel ran his hand through his hair. "My father didn't approve. He thought Thomas was wasting his time. He wanted him to focus on the business. On management. Not on getting his hands dirty."

"But Thomas didn't listen."

"No. He kept going to that shop. Learning. Working." Nathaniel smiled sadly. "He used to come home with ink on his fingers. Oil under his nails. My father hated it. But Thomas didn't care. He said real skill came from doing. Not from watching."

Clara's throat felt tight. She knew she should stay quiet. But the words came out anyway. "What happened to him?"

Nathaniel's expression darkened. "There was an accident. At the factory. Part of the floor collapsed. Thomas was working late. He fell three storeys."

"That's terrible."

"The official report said it was poor maintenance. Rotten boards. No one's fault." Nathaniel looked at her. His eyes were full of pain. "But Thomas didn't believe in accidents. He used to say that every failure has a cause. Something someone did or didn't do."

Clara didn't know what to say. The weight of the secret pressed on her. Her father had trained Thomas. She was sure of it now. The timing fit. The description fit. Everything fit.

And her father had warned her away from the Blackwoods. Because of what happened to Thomas? Because he blamed them?

"I'm sorry for your loss," Clara said quietly.

"It was a long time ago."

"That doesn't make it easier."

"No." Nathaniel looked at the watches on the bench. "Sometimes I think about what Thomas would have done. If he had lived. If he had taken over the factory. He would have changed things. Made them better. More humane."

"You could still do that."

"Could I?" Nathaniel's voice was bitter. "My father controls everything. The factory. The workers. The designs. I'm just a figurehead. Someone to sign papers and attend meetings."

"You're more than that."

"Am I?" Nathaniel looked at her. "What do you see when you look at me, Clara?"

The question surprised her. Clara thought about it. Really thought about it.

"I see someone who cares," she said finally. "Someone who wants to do the right thing. Even when it's difficult."

Nathaniel was quiet. Then he said, "My brother would have liked you."

"Would he?"

"Yes. You remind me of him. The way you talk about watches. The passion. The precision." Nathaniel smiled. "He used to say that watchmaking was about more than keeping time. It was about creating something that lasted. Something that mattered."

Clara felt her eyes sting. She blinked quickly. "That's beautiful."

"He was beautiful. In his way." Nathaniel stood. "I should let you get back to work."

"Wait." Clara picked up her sketch. The modified escapement. "Take this. Use it. If you want."

Nathaniel took the paper. He looked at it for a long moment. "This is good work."

"It's just an idea."

"It's more than that." Nathaniel folded the paper carefully and put it in his pocket. "Thank you."

He moved towards the door. Clara found herself not wanting him to leave. The conversation had felt real. Honest. Different from the careful politeness they usually maintained.

"Mr. Blackwood?"

He turned. "Yes?"

Clara wanted to tell him. About her father. About Thomas. About the connection between them.

But the words wouldn't come. The risk was too great.

"Nothing," she said. "Just... thank you. For asking my opinion."

Nathaniel smiled. "I should be thanking you. You've given me a lot to think about."

He left. Clara stood alone in the small room. Her heart was racing. Her hands were shaking.

She sat down at the bench and picked up one of the watches. She needed to focus. To work. To stop thinking about Nathaniel's sad eyes and kind words.

But she couldn't.

She kept thinking about Thomas. About her father. About secrets and lies and all the things left unsaid.

Clara set the watch down and closed her eyes. A memory came to her. She was seven years old. Standing in her father's shop. A young man was there. Bent over the workbench. Her father stood beside him, showing him how to clean a gear.

"Gently," her father had said. "Like you're holding something precious."

The young man had looked up. He had seen Clara watching from the doorway. He had smiled.

"Is this your daughter?" he had asked.

"Yes. Clara."

"Hello, Clara." The young man had waved. His hands were covered in oil. "Do you like watches?"

Clara had nodded shyly.

"Me too." The young man had gone back to his work. "Your father is teaching me. He's very patient. Very kind."

"My father is the best watchmaker in Birmingham," Clara had said proudly.

The young man had laughed. "I believe it."

That had been Thomas. Clara was certain now. He had come to learn from her father. And her father had taught him.

And then Thomas had died. And everything had changed.

Clara opened her eyes. The memory faded but the feeling remained. Sadness. Loss. Connection.

She thought about Nathaniel. About the way he talked about his brother. The love in his voice. The pain.

And she thought about the moment just before he left. When he had looked at her. Really looked at her.

Something had passed between them. Something unspoken. A recognition. An understanding.

Clara touched her chest. Her heart was beating too fast. She felt warm. Confused.

This was dangerous. More dangerous than hiding her identity. More dangerous than working in secret.

Because she was starting to care about Nathaniel Blackwood. Not as an employer. Not as a customer. As a person.

And that could ruin everything.

Clara stood and paced the small room. She needed to be careful. To maintain distance. To remember why she was here.

For the money. For her father. For the shop.

Not for anything else. Certainly not for feelings.

But even as she told herself this, she knew it was too late. Something had shifted. Something had changed.

The door opened. Clara turned, expecting Mr. Pell or another worker.

It was Nathaniel. He stood in the doorway, breathing slightly hard. Like he had been running.

"I forgot something," he said.

"What?"

Nathaniel stepped into the room and closed the door. He crossed to the bench. He stood close to her. Closer than was proper.

"I wanted to tell you something," he said. "About what you said. About me caring. About wanting to do the right thing."

Clara could barely breathe. "Yes?"

"You're the first person who's seen that in a long time. The first person who's looked past the name. Past the family. Past all of it." Nathaniel's voice was low. Intense. "And I wanted you to know that I see you too. Not just as a worker. Not just as a skilled craftsman. As someone remarkable."

Clara's face burned. She didn't know where to look. What to say.

"I should go," Nathaniel said quickly. "I'm sorry. That was inappropriate."

"No." The word came out before Clara could stop it. "It wasn't."

They stood there. Inches apart. The air between them felt charged. Electric.

Nathaniel lifted his hand. For a moment Clara thought he might touch her. Her face. Her hand. Something.

But he didn't. He let his hand fall. Stepped back.

"I should go," he said again. "I have a meeting."

"Of course."

Nathaniel moved to the door. He paused with his hand on the handle. He looked back at her.

Their eyes met. Held.

Then he left.

Clara stood frozen. Her heart pounded. Her skin felt too hot. Her mind raced.

What had just happened? What did it mean?

She sat down at the bench. Her legs felt weak.

This was exactly what she had feared. What she had tried to avoid.

She was falling for Nathaniel Blackwood. And he might be falling for her.

And that could destroy them both.

Chapter Nine

CLARA NEEDED A SMALLER file. The one she had been using at the factory was too coarse for the delicate work she wanted to do. She knew her father had one somewhere in the shop. She just had to find it.

It was Sunday. Her one day away from the factory. Clara had spent the morning cleaning the shop and checking on her father. He had been sleeping more lately. Sometimes he barely woke at all.

Now she stood in the workshop and looked around. Her father's tools were scattered everywhere. Some on the bench. Some in drawers. Some in boxes stacked in the corner.

Clara opened drawer after drawer. She found old gears. Springs. Broken cases. But no small file.

She moved to the boxes in the corner. Most of them were light. Filled with scraps and spare parts. But one box was heavier. It sat at the bottom of the stack.

Clara pulled it out and set it on the bench. It was made of dark wood. Old. Well made. A small brass lock held it closed.

She had never seen this box before.

Clara tried the lock. It held firm. She looked around for a key but found nothing.

She should leave it alone. Put it back. It was locked for a reason.

But curiosity nagged at her. What was inside? Why had her father locked it away?

Clara picked up a thin tool. She worked it into the lock carefully. After a few minutes, the lock clicked open.

She lifted the lid.

Inside were papers. Letters. Documents. And at the bottom, a leather-bound journal.

Clara's hands trembled as she lifted the journal out. The leather was worn. The edges soft with age. She opened it to the first page.

Her father's handwriting. Neat and precise. Dated fifteen years ago.

Clara sat down on the stool and began to read.

The first entries were ordinary. Notes about repairs. Sketches of designs. Lists of supplies needed.

Then the tone changed.

April 12, 1860

"Thomas Blackwood visited again today. Bright young man. Eager to learn. His father does not approve. Says watchmaking is beneath him. But Thomas loves the craft. I see it in his eyes."

Clara's breath caught. Thomas. Nathaniel's brother. Her father had written about him.

She turned the page.

May 3, 1860

"Thomas brought me a design today. An improved escapement. Elegant. Efficient. Better than anything I have seen. I told him it was brilliant. He wants to show it to his father. I advised caution. The elder Blackwood has a reputation."

Clara read faster now. Entry after entry about Thomas. About his visits to the shop. About his designs. His passion for watchmaking.

Then the entries grew darker.

August 20, 1860

"Thomas came to the shop today. He was upset. Angry. He said his father took one of his designs. A new balance wheel. Thomas showed it to him in confidence. Now the factory is producing watches with that exact design. No credit given. No acknowledgment."

"I told Thomas to be careful. The elder Blackwood is not a man to cross. But Thomas wants justice. He says his father has done this before. Stolen designs from others. Built the family fortune on the backs of true craftsmen."

Clara's hands were shaking. She turned the page.

September 15, 1860

"Thomas has proof. He found letters. Documents. Evidence that his father paid workers to steal designs from other workshops. My designs among t hem.""*I looked through my old records. Thomas is right. Three of my best designs appeared in Blackwood watches within months of my creating them. I thought it was coincidence. Now I know better."

"Thomas wants to expose his father. I warned him against it. The Blackwoods have power. Money. Influence. What chance does one young man have against that?"

Clara felt sick. Her father's designs. Stolen. Used without permission or payment. That was why the shop had failed. Why they had lost everything.

She kept reading.

November 2, 1860

"Thomas has not been to the shop in weeks. I am worried. I sent a message to the Blackwood house. No reply."

December 10, 1860

"I heard the news today. Thomas Blackwood is dead. A factory accident, they say. He fell three storeys. Died instantly."

"But I do not believe in accidents. Not when they happen to young men who ask too many questions. Who threaten powerful families."

"I went to the factory. Asked to see the site of the accident. They refused. Said it was under investigation. But there will be no real investigation. The Blackwoods own the police. Own the inspectors. Own everyone who matters."

"Thomas tried to do the right thing. He tried to expose the truth. And it killed him."

Clara's eyes burned. She blinked hard. The words on the page blurred.

Thomas had known. He had found evidence. He had tried to tell the truth.

And he had died for it.

She turned to the next entry.

January 5, 1861

"The official report came out today. Accident. Poor maintenance. No one to blame."

"But I know better. I know what Thomas found. I know what he was going to do."

"And I am afraid. Afraid for Clara. Afraid for myself. Afraid of what the Blackwoods might do if they think I know too much."

"I have decided to say nothing. To do nothing. To protect my daughter. Even if it means letting Thomas's death go unpunished."

"I am a coward. God forgive me."

The entries stopped after that. The rest of the pages were blank.

Clara closed the journal. She sat in silence. Her mind raced.

Her father had known. All this time, he had known. Known that Thomas was murdered. Known that the Blackwoods were thieves and possibly worse.

And he had said nothing. To protect her.

Clara stood and paced the workshop. Her hands clenched into fists.

Nathaniel. She thought about him. About his kindness. His sadness when he talked about Thomas. His frustration with his father.

Did he know? Did he suspect?

Clara didn't think so. Nathaniel seemed genuinely haunted by his brother's death. Genuinely confused about what had happened.

But his father. The elder Blackwood. He knew. He had to know.

Clara felt anger burning in her chest. Hot and fierce. Thomas had died trying to do the right thing. And the man responsible was still in power. Still running the factory. Still pretending to be respectable.

She thought about her own father. About the guilt he carried. About the fear that had consumed him for fifteen years.

No wonder he had warned her away from the Blackwoods. No wonder he had been so angry when she told him about the commission.

He was trying to protect her. The way he had failed to protect Thomas.

Clara looked at the journal in her hands. This was evidence. Proof that Thomas had been investigating his father. That he had found something damaging.

But was it enough? Could she use it to expose the truth?

Clara sat back down and opened the journal again. She read through the entries more carefully this time. Looking for details. Names. Dates. Anything that could be verified.

Her father mentioned letters. Documents. Evidence that Thomas had found. But where was it? Did it still exist?

Or had the elder Blackwood destroyed it all?

Clara closed the journal and held it against her chest. She felt torn. Part of her wanted to march into the factory and confront Nathaniel. Tell him everything. Show him the journal. Demand justice for Thomas.

But another part of her was afraid. Afraid of what would happen if she spoke out. Afraid of losing her position at the factory. Afraid of putting herself and her father in danger.

And underneath it all was something else. Something more complicated.

She cared about Nathaniel. She had started to trust him. Maybe even to have feelings for him.

How could she tell him that his father was a murderer? That his family's fortune was built on theft and lies?

It would destroy him. Or worse, he might not believe her. He might think she was lying. Making false accusations to hurt the Blackwood name.

Clara stood and paced again. She felt trapped. Caught between loyalty to her father, justice for Thomas, and her growing attachment to Nathaniel.

She thought about Thomas's last days. About how he must have felt. Knowing the truth. Wanting to expose it. Fearing what might happen if he did.

And then he died. And the truth died with him.

Except it didn't. Because her father had written it down. Had kept a record. Had preserved Thomas's story.

Clara looked at the journal again. Her father had been afraid. Too afraid to act. Too afraid to seek justice.

But Clara was not her father. She was younger. Stronger. Braver.

And she had something her father never had. She had access to Nathaniel. To someone inside the Blackwood family who might listen. Who might care.

But how could she tell him? How could she show him this journal without revealing who she really was?

Because if Nathaniel knew she was C. Wren, knew she was the daughter of the watchmaker who had trained Thomas, he would connect the pieces. He would understand why she was working at the factory. Why she had hidden her identity.

And he might see it as deception. As manipulation. As an attempt to get close to him for revenge.

Clara sat back down. Her head ached. Her heart ached.

She had thought working at the factory would be simple. Earn money. Prove her skill. Keep her secrets.

But nothing was simple anymore. Everything was complicated. Tangled up in old grievances and new feelings and secrets that stretched back years.

Clara opened the journal one more time. She read the last entry again.

I am a coward. God forgive me.

Her father had called himself a coward. But he was not. He was a father trying to protect his daughter. A man trying to survive in a world that had crushed him.

But what was Clara? What would she do with this knowledge?

She thought about Nathaniel's face when he talked about Thomas. The love. The loss. The unanswered questions.

He deserved to know the truth. Thomas deserved to be remembered for what he really was. A hero. Someone who tried to do the right thing.

But telling the truth meant risking everything. Her job. Her safety. Her future.

And maybe her heart.

Clara closed the journal and held it tight. She would have to decide. Soon.

But not today. Today she needed to think. To plan. To figure out how to tell the truth without destroying everything she had built.

She put the journal back in the box. But she did not lock it. She left it on the bench. Where she could see it. Where it would remind her of what was at stake.

Then she went upstairs to check on her father.

He was awake. Sitting up in bed. He looked at her with tired eyes.

"Clara. Is something wrong? You look upset."

Clara sat on the edge of the bed. She wanted to tell him. To show him what she had found. To ask him what to do.

But she could not. He was too weak. Too fragile. The knowledge that she had found the journal might break him.

"I'm fine, Papa. Just tired."

"You work too hard." He reached for her hand. "Promise me you'll be careful. At that factory. With those people."

"I promise."

"The Blackwoods are dangerous, Clara. Never forget that."

"I won't."

Her father squeezed her hand. Then he lay back against the pillows and closed his eyes.

Clara sat with him until he fell asleep. Then she went back downstairs to the workshop.

The box sat on the bench. Waiting.

Clara opened it again. She took out the journal. She held it in her hands.

This was truth. This was proof. This was justice waiting to be claimed.

But it was also dangerous. Explosive. Something that could hurt everyone involved.

Clara thought about Nathaniel. About the moment in the factory when he had looked at her and called her remarkable. About the electricity between them. About the feelings growing in her chest.

Could she risk losing that? Could she risk pushing him away by telling him his father was a monster?

But could she keep silent? Could she let Thomas's death remain unavenged? Could she let the elder

Blackwood continue to prosper while her own father withered away in guilt and fear?

Clara did not know. She truly did not know.

She closed the journal and put it back in the box. She would keep it safe. Keep it hidden. Until she decided what to do.

But she knew one thing for certain.

The truth would come out. Eventually. Whether she wanted it to or not.

Because secrets this big never stayed buried forever.

And when the truth finally emerged, it would change everything.

Clara looked at the box one last time. Then she pushed it back into the corner. Under the other boxes. Out of sight.

But not out of mind. Never out of mind.

The truth was there. Waiting.

And Clara would have to decide what to do with it.

Chapter Ten

C LARA ARRIVED AT THE factory on Monday morning with the weight of her father's journal still heavy in her mind. She had barely slept. Every time she closed her eyes, she saw the words. Thomas Blackwood. Stolen designs. Murder.

She walked through the factory gates and kept her head down. The fewer people who noticed her, the better.

She reached her small room and closed the door behind her. The familiar sound of the factory surrounded her. Hammering. Grinding. The roar of machinery. Usually it comforted her. Today it felt oppressive.

Clara hung up her shawl and put on her work apron. She had a box of old mechanisms to sort through. Simple work. Mindless work. Exactly what she needed.

She opened the box and began laying out parts on the bench. Springs. Gears. Screws. She sorted them by size and type.

An hour passed. Then another. Clara lost herself in the work. Her hands moved automatically. Her mind drifted.

The door opened. Clara looked up. Mr. Pell stood in the doorway. His expression was serious.

"Clara. Mr. Blackwood wants to see you. In his office."

Clara's stomach dropped. "Now?"

"Yes. Come along."

Clara set down her tools and followed Mr. Pell through the corridors. Workers stared at her as she passed. Some whispered. Clara felt their eyes on her back.

Something was wrong.

They reached Nathaniel's office. Mr. Pell knocked and opened the door. "She's here, sir."

"Thank you, Pell. You may go."

Mr. Pell left. Clara stepped into the office. Nathaniel stood behind his desk. He looked tired. Troubled.

But he was not alone.

Basil Thorn stood by the window. His arms were crossed. His expression was cold. Triumphant.

"Close the door," Nathaniel said quietly.

Clara closed it. Her heart pounded.

"Sit down, Clara."

She sat. Her hands gripped the edge of the chair.

Nathaniel looked at her for a long moment. Then he said, "Something has gone missing from the factory. A valuable part. A custom-made gear for one of our most important clients."

Clara's mouth went dry. "I don't understand."

"The gear was in the parts room yesterday morning. By afternoon, it was gone." Nathaniel's voice was careful. Controlled. "Several workers reported seeing you near the parts room yesterday."

"I was looking for supplies. Mr. Pell sent me."

"That may be." Basil stepped forward. His voice was smooth. Dangerous. "But the fact remains. The gear is missing. And you were the last person seen in that area."

Clara looked at Nathaniel. "You think I stole it?"

"I don't know what to think." Nathaniel's jaw was tight. "I'm trying to understand what happened."

"I didn't take anything. I wouldn't."

"Then where is it?" Basil moved closer. Too close. Clara could smell the oil on his clothes. "That gear is worth more than you make in a month. Maybe you thought you could sell it. Pay off some debts."

"I didn't steal anything."

"So you say." Basil smiled. It was not a pleasant smile. "But we only have your word for that. And you're just a temporary worker. A nobody. Why should we believe you?"

"That's enough, Basil." Nathaniel's voice was sharp.

"Is it?" Basil turned to Nathaniel. "This girl appears out of nowhere. You give her special treatment. Private workspace. Access to valuable parts. And now something goes missing. I warned you. I told you this would happen."

"Nothing has been proven."

"Nothing needs to be proven. The part is gone. She was there. Fire her and be done with it."

Clara stood. Her legs felt weak but she forced herself to stay upright. "I understand how this looks. But I did not take that gear. I have never stolen anything in my life."

Nathaniel looked at her. His eyes searched her face. Looking for what? Truth? Lies?

"I want to believe you," he said quietly.

"Then believe me."

"It's not that simple." Nathaniel moved around his desk. "The client who ordered that gear is important. Powerful. If we don't deliver, we lose the contract. My father will demand answers."

"Then find the real thief."

"Oh, please." Basil laughed. It was a harsh sound. "You expect us to waste time searching for some imaginary culprit? While you walk free? No. You're dismissed. Pack your things and leave."

"You don't have the authority to dismiss her." Nathaniel's voice was cold.

"Don't I?" Basil's eyes narrowed. "I'm the factory foreman. I'm responsible for discipline. And I say she goes."

"And I say we investigate first."

The two men stared at each other. The air between them crackled with tension.

Finally Basil said, "Fine. Investigate. But while you're wasting time, I'll be reporting this to your father. Let's see what he thinks about your special worker."

Basil walked out. He slammed the door behind him.

Clara and Nathaniel stood in silence. The noise of the factory filtered through the walls. Distant. Muffled.

"I didn't take it," Clara said again. Her voice was steady but her hands shook. "I swear to you."

Nathaniel sank into his chair. He rubbed his face with both hands. "I believe you."

"Do you?"

"Yes." He looked up at her. "But belief isn't enough. I need proof. Something concrete. Otherwise Basil will go to my father. And my father will side with him."

"What can I do?"

"Go back to your room. Work as normal. Don't speak to anyone about this. I'll search the parts room. Question the workers. Find out what really happened."

Clara nodded. But she felt hopeless. Someone had stolen the gear and made it look like her fault. And she knew exactly who.

Basil Thorn.

He had been watching her since the day she arrived. Suspicious. Jealous. Determined to get rid of her.

This was his opportunity. And he was taking it.

Clara walked to the door. She paused with her hand on the handle. "Mr. Blackwood?"

"Yes?"

"Even if you find proof that I'm innocent, Basil won't stop. He wants me gone. He'll find another way."

Nathaniel was quiet for a moment. Then he said, "Let me worry about Basil."

Clara left the office. She walked back through the corridors. Workers still stared. Still whispered. Word had spread quickly.

The new girl is a thief.

She reached her room and closed the door. She leaned against it and took a deep breath.

She had been accused of theft. If she could not prove her innocence, she would be fired. Maybe worse. Maybe arrested.

And all because Basil wanted to hurt Nathaniel. Because she had become a weapon in their rivalry.

Clara sat at her bench. She tried to work. But her hands would not cooperate. They shook too much.

An hour passed. Then the door opened.

Mr. Pell entered. His face was kind but worried. "How are you holding up?"

"Not well."

"I don't believe you took that gear."

"Thank you."

Mr. Pell closed the door and moved closer. He lowered his voice. "I've been at this factory for thirty years. I've seen a lot. And I know Basil Thorn. He's ambitious. Ruthless. He doesn't like that Mr. Blackwood favours you."

"I know."

"Be careful, Clara. Basil doesn't fight fair. And he has friends. Powerful friends."

"What should I do?"

Mr. Pell hesitated. Then he said, "There's a broken regulator in the workshop. Third floor. No one's been able to fix it. If you could repair it, it might help. Show your value. Give Mr. Blackwood a reason to keep you."

"Will it make a difference?"

"It might. It's all I can think of."

Mr. Pell left. Clara sat in silence.

A broken regulator. A chance to prove herself. It was something. Not much. But something.

Clara stood and left her room. She climbed the stairs to the third floor. The noise was louder here. The machinery heavier. Men worked at benches, barely looking up as she passed.

She found the workshop Mr. Pell had mentioned. The broken regulator sat on a shelf. Dusty. Neglected.

Clara picked it up and examined it. The mechanism was complex. Delicate. The kind of work that required patience and skill.

She could fix it. She was sure of that.

But first she had to get it back to her room without anyone noticing.

Clara tucked the regulator under her arm and walked quickly back down the stairs. She passed workers. Supervisors. No one stopped her. No one asked what she was carrying.

She reached her room and set the regulator on her bench. Then she locked the door.

For the next three hours, Clara worked. She took the regulator apart piece by piece. Cleaned each component. Identified the problems. A bent spring. A misaligned gear. A worn bearing.

She fixed them one by one. Slowly. Carefully. Her hands stopped shaking. Her mind focused.

This was what she knew. This was what she was good at.

Finally, she reassembled the regulator. She wound it. Tested it.

It worked. Perfectly.

Clara set it down and allowed herself a small smile. Whatever happened with the missing gear, at least she had this. Proof that she could do good work. That she was valuable.

A knock at the door made her jump.

"Come in."

Nathaniel entered. His expression was carefully neutral.

"Have you found anything?" Clara asked.

"Yes." Nathaniel closed the door behind him. "The missing gear. It was in the parts locker on the second floor. Hidden behind some old screws."

Clara's heart leapt. "So you know I didn't take it."

"I know someone put it there to make you look guilty."

"It was Basil."

"I can't prove that. The locker is accessible to dozens of workers."

"But you know it was him."

Nathaniel sighed. "Knowing and proving are different things. Basil is careful. He covers his tracks."

Clara felt the hope drain out of her. "So what happens now?"

"Now I tell my father the gear has been found. That there was a mistake. No theft. Just a misplaced part."

"Will he believe that?"

"He'll have to. I'm not firing you based on Basil's word alone."

Clara picked up the regulator. "I fixed this. While I was waiting. Mr. Pell said no one else could repair it."

Nathaniel took the regulator. He examined it. Tested it. His expression changed. Softened.

"This is remarkable work."

"I needed to do something useful."

Nathaniel set the regulator down. He looked at her. Really looked at her. "You didn't deserve this. What Basil did. The accusation. The humiliation."

"No. I didn't."

"I'm sorry."

"It's not your fault."

"Isn't it?" Nathaniel moved closer. "I brought you here. I put you in this position. I made you a target."

"I chose to come. I knew the risks."

"Did you? Did you know that Basil would try to destroy you? That the workers would whisper and judge? That I wouldn't be able to protect you?"

Clara met his eyes. "I knew enough."

They stood in silence. The air between them felt heavy. Charged.

Nathaniel reached out. His hand almost touched her arm. Then he pulled back.

"I want to keep you safe," he said quietly. "But I don't know how."

"You found the gear. You proved I didn't steal it. That's enough."

"Is it?" Nathaniel's voice was bitter. "Basil will try again. He won't stop until you're gone."

"Then I'll be more careful."

"Clara..." Nathaniel stopped. He seemed to struggle with something. Then he said, "Why do you stay? After everything that's happened. The accusations. The danger. Why not just leave?"

Clara thought about the journal. About Thomas. About the truth she carried but could not speak.

She thought about her father. Dying slowly in his bed. Consumed by guilt and fear.

She thought about the money. About the shop. About survival.

But most of all, she thought about Nathaniel. About the way he looked at her. About the moments between them that felt like something more.

"I stay because the work matters," Clara said finally. "And because I'm not ready to give up."

Nathaniel nodded slowly. "Neither am I."

He picked up the regulator. "I'll take this to the workshop. Show them what you did. Make sure everyone knows."

"Thank you."

"Don't thank me. You did the work." Nathaniel moved to the door. He paused. "Clara? Be careful. Basil is dangerous. More dangerous than you realise."

"I know."

Nathaniel left. Clara sat down at her bench. Her whole body felt heavy. Exhausted.

The accusation. The confrontation. The hours of work. It had drained her.

But she had survived. She had proven herself. Again.

And Nathaniel had stood by her. He had investigated. Found the truth. Defended her.

That meant something.

Clara thought about the journal hidden in her shop. About the secrets it contained. About the choice she would eventually have to make.

Tell Nathaniel the truth. Or keep silent.

Both options felt impossible. Both would hurt someone.

But for now, she would keep working. Keep surviving. Keep pretending that everything was normal.

Even though nothing was normal anymore.

Even though danger surrounded her on all sides.

Even though she knew, deep down, that this was only the beginning.

Basil had made his move. And he had failed. But he would try again. Harder. Worse.

And next time, Clara might not be so lucky.

She looked at the door Nathaniel had just walked through. She thought about his words. About the concern in his voice. About the way he had almost touched her.

Something was growing between them. Something real. Something that frightened her as much as it thrilled her.

But it was also dangerous. Because the closer they became, the harder it would be to keep her secrets.

And when those secrets finally came out, they would destroy everything.

Clara knew that. She had always known that.

But still, she stayed.

Because she was not ready to give up on the work. On the factory. On the small space where she had proven herself.

And she was not ready to give up on Nathaniel. On whatever was building between them.

Even if it meant risking everything.

Even if it meant facing Basil's wrath again and again.

Clara picked up her tools and went back to work.

One piece at a time. One repair at a time. One day at a time.

That was all she could do.

That was all anyone could do.

And maybe, if she was careful enough, skilled enough, brave enough, it would be enough to survive.

Chapter Eleven

THREE DAYS AFTER THE incident with the missing gear, Nathaniel came to Clara's room in the middle of the afternoon. She was sorting through a box of springs when he knocked.

"Come in."

Nathaniel entered and closed the door behind him. He looked uncomfortable. Nervous, even. Clara had never seen him nervous before.

"Is something wrong?" she asked.

"No. Nothing's wrong." Nathaniel stayed near the door. "I wanted to ask you something. It's rather... unconventional."

Clara set down the spring she was holding. "What is it?"

"The factory holds a winter gathering every year. For the managers and their families. Some of the senior workers. A dinner and dancing." Nathaniel paused. "It's next Saturday evening."

Clara waited. She did not understand why he was telling her this.

"I would like you to attend. As my guest."

Clara's heart skipped. "What?"

"I know it's unusual. You're not a manager. You're not family. But you've done good work here. Important work. I think you deserve recognition."

Clara stood slowly. "Mr. Blackwood, I don't think that's wise."

"Why not?"

"Because people will talk. They already whisper about me. About why you've given me special treatment. If I attend as your guest, it will only make things worse."

"I don't care what people say."

"Maybe you don't. But I do." Clara's voice was quiet but firm. "I have to work here. I have to face these people every day. Making me more visible, more noticeable, will only cause problems."

Nathaniel moved closer. "You shouldn't have to hide, Clara. You're talented. Skilled. You deserve to be seen."

"But not like this. Not as your guest at a formal gathering. It would be... inappropriate."

"Why? Because you're a woman?"

Clara felt her face flush. "Because I'm just a temporary worker. Because it would raise questions I can't answer."

Nathaniel was quiet for a moment. Then he said, "What if I told you I want you there? Not because of your work. Not because you deserve recognition. But because I want to spend an evening with you."

Clara's breath caught. The words hung in the air between them.

"Mr. Blackwood..."

"Nathaniel. Please. Call me Nathaniel."

"That wouldn't be proper."

"Neither is this conversation. But I'm having it anyway." Nathaniel's eyes met hers. "I'm asking you to come. Not as a worker. As my guest. Please."

Clara knew she should say no. She should refuse. It was dangerous. It would expose her to scrutiny. To questions. To Basil's suspicion.

But part of her wanted to say yes. Wanted to spend an evening away from the factory floor. Away from the noise and grime. Wanted to wear something other than her grey work dress. Wanted to be seen as something other than a nameless worker.

Wanted to be with Nathaniel. In a setting where they could talk. Dance. Be something more than employer and employee.

"I don't have anything suitable to wear," Clara said finally.

Nathaniel smiled. "Is that a yes?"

"It's a practical concern."

"But not a refusal."

Clara looked away. "I would need to borrow a gown. From my cousin. And I would need to tell my father something. Some excuse for why I'll be out that evening."

"So you'll come?"

Clara met his eyes again. She saw hope there. Warmth. Something that made her chest feel tight.

"Yes. I'll come."

Nathaniel's smile widened. "Good. The gathering starts at seven. I'll send a carriage for you. Where should it pick you up?"

Clara gave him her address at the shop. The words felt dangerous. Like she was giving away too much. But it was too late now. She had agreed.

After Nathaniel left, Clara sat down at her bench. Her hands were shaking. What had she just done?

That evening, Clara went to see Lizzy at the dressmaker's shop. Her cousin was just finishing for the day when Clara arrived.

"Clara!" Lizzy's face lit up. "What a lovely surprise. What brings you here?"

"I need your help."

"Of course. What is it?"

Clara glanced around. The shop was empty except for them. "I need to borrow a gown. For Saturday evening."

Lizzy's eyes widened. "A gown? Why? What's happening on Saturday?"

"I've been invited to a gathering. At the factory."

"A gathering? Clara, that's wonderful!" Lizzy grabbed her hands. "Who invited you?"

"Mr. Blackwood. The owner's son."

Lizzy squealed. Actually squealed. Clara shushed her quickly.

"Lizzy, please. This isn't... it's just a work event."

"Is it?" Lizzy's eyes sparkled with mischief. "Because it sounds like more than that to me. He invited you specifically. As his guest."

"It's complicated."

"It always is." Lizzy pulled Clara towards the back room. "Come on. Let's find you something beautiful."

Lizzy had several gowns. Hand-me-downs from wealthy clients. Dresses that had gone out of fashion or needed alterations the clients never collected.

She pulled out a dark blue gown. Simple but elegant. No excessive lace or frills. Just clean lines and good fabric.

"Try this one."

Clara changed behind the screen. The gown fit reasonably well. A little loose in the waist but Lizzy could fix that.

Clara looked at herself in the mirror. She barely recognised the person staring back. The girl in the reflection looked grown up. Refined. Like someone who belonged at a formal gathering.

"You look beautiful," Lizzy said softly.

"I look strange."

"You look like yourself. Just dressed properly for once." Lizzy adjusted the sleeves. "This Mr. Blackwood. Do you like him?"

Clara hesitated. "I respect him."

"That's not what I asked."

"Lizzy..."

"Clara, you wouldn't be this nervous about a work event. And you certainly wouldn't be borrowing a gown just to impress your employer." Lizzy turned Clara to face her. "Do you like him?"

Clara thought about Nathaniel. About his kindness. His intelligence. The way he listened when she spoke. The way he looked at her sometimes.

"I don't know," she said quietly. "Maybe."

"Then go to this gathering. Enjoy yourself. Dance with him. See what happens."

"Nothing can happen. There are too many secrets. Too many lies."

"Maybe it's time to tell the truth."

Clara shook her head. "I can't. Not yet."

"Then when?"

Clara didn't have an answer.

Saturday evening came too quickly. Clara spent the afternoon getting ready. She bathed carefully. Washed and dried her hair. Let Lizzy come over to help her dress and arrange her hair.

Her father watched from his chair. He looked worried.

"Where did you say you were going?" he asked.

"A small gathering. Some of the people from the factory. To celebrate the winter season."

"And this Mr. Blackwood will be there?"

"Yes, Papa."

Her father was quiet. Then he said, "Be careful, Clara. These people... they're not like us. They have money. Power. They can be kind one moment and cruel the next."

"I know."

"Do you?" Her father reached for her hand. "Promise me you'll be careful. Promise me you won't let them hurt you."

"I promise."

At quarter to seven, a carriage arrived. Clara kissed her father goodbye and went outside. The carriage was elegant. Well maintained. The driver helped her inside.

The journey to the factory took twenty minutes. Clara's stomach churned the entire way. What was she doing? This was madness.

The carriage stopped outside a large building next to the factory. Clara had never noticed it before. Light spilled from the windows. She could hear music. Voices. Laughter.

The driver helped her down. Clara smoothed her gown and took a deep breath.

She could do this. She had to do this.

She walked up the steps and entered the building. The entrance hall was decorated with greenery and candles. It looked warm. Inviting.

A man stood near the doorway. Checking names. Clara approached nervously.

"Your name, miss?"

"Clara. I'm... I'm Mr. Blackwood's guest."

The man checked his list. His eyebrows rose slightly. But he nodded. "Of course. Through there."

Clara walked through into a large room. It was beautiful. High ceilings. Polished floors. Tables laden with food. A small orchestra played in the corner.

People filled the room. Well-dressed men and women. Talking. Laughing. Drinking. Clara felt immediately out of place.

She stood near the door. Uncertain. Looking for Nathaniel.

"Clara."

She turned. Nathaniel stood behind her. He wore a formal suit. His hair was neatly combed. He looked handsome. More handsome than Clara had ever seen him.

"You came," he said.

"I did."

"You look..." Nathaniel stopped. Seemed to search for words. "Beautiful."

Clara's face warmed. "Thank you. You look very fine yourself."

Nathaniel offered his arm. "May I?"

Clara hesitated. Then she took his arm. They walked into the room together.

Immediately, Clara felt eyes on them. People turned. Stared. Whispered.

A woman in an expensive gown leaned towards her companion. Clara heard fragments of the conversation. "Who is she?" "Never seen her before." "Rather plain, isn't she?"

Clara's face burned. She wanted to turn around. To leave. But Nathaniel's arm was firm under her hand.

"Ignore them," he said quietly.

"They're staring."

"Let them."

Across the room, Clara saw Basil Thorn. He stood with a group of men. His face darkened when he saw her. His eyes narrowed.

Clara looked away quickly.

Nathaniel led her to a quiet corner. He fetched her a glass of wine. Clara had never tasted wine before. It was sharp. Strange. But warming.

"Are you all right?" Nathaniel asked.

"I feel like everyone is watching me."

"They are. But not for the reasons you think." Nathaniel leaned closer. "They're watching because you're with me. Because I've never brought anyone to these gatherings before. They're curious."

"And Basil? Why is he watching?"

Nathaniel glanced across the room. Basil was still staring at them. His expression was cold. Calculating.

"Basil is always watching. Looking for opportunities. Weaknesses." Nathaniel turned back to Clara. "Don't worry about him. Tonight is about us. Not him."

The music changed. A waltz began. Couples moved onto the dance floor.

Nathaniel set down his glass. "Will you dance with me?"

Clara's heart raced. "I don't know how."

"I'll teach you. It's simple."

"Nathaniel, I..."

"Please."

Clara looked at the dance floor. At the couples moving gracefully across the polished wood. She would look foolish. She would make mistakes. People would laugh.

But Nathaniel was looking at her with such hope. Such warmth.

"All right," she said quietly.

Nathaniel led her onto the floor. He placed one hand on her waist. The other held her hand gently. Clara's breath caught at the touch.

"Follow my lead," Nathaniel said. "Left foot back. Now right foot to the side. Now close."

Clara stumbled at first. She stepped on his foot once. Twice. But Nathaniel just smiled and kept leading.

Gradually, Clara found the rhythm. Her feet moved more smoothly. Her body relaxed. She looked up at Nathaniel and found him watching her.

"You're doing well," he said.

"You're a good teacher."

They moved across the floor. Around them, other couples danced. But Clara barely noticed. She was aware only of Nathaniel. Of his hand on her waist. Of his eyes on her face. Of the music surrounding them.

For a few minutes, everything else faded. The secrets. The lies. The danger. All of it fell away. There was only this moment. This dance. This feeling.

The music ended. The couples stopped. Applause filled the room.

Nathaniel and Clara stood still for a moment. Neither moved. Neither spoke.

Then Nathaniel said quietly, "Would you like some air?"

Clara nodded. Words seemed impossible.

Nathaniel led her through the room. Past the staring guests. Past Basil's cold glare. Out through a door onto a small balcony.

The night air was cold. Sharp. Clara shivered and Nathaniel removed his jacket, draping it over her shoulders.

"Better?" he asked.

"Yes. Thank you."

They stood in silence. Looking out over the factory yard. The smoke. The darkness beyond.

"I'm glad you came tonight," Nathaniel said.

"So am I."

"I know it was difficult. Coming here. Being seen."

"It was. But it was also..." Clara searched for the right word. "Wonderful."

Nathaniel turned to face her. "Clara, I need to tell you something."

Clara's heart hammered. "What?"

"These past weeks. Working with you. Talking with you. I've..." Nathaniel stopped. Seemed to struggle. "I've come to care for you. More than I should. More than is appropriate."

Clara couldn't breathe. The words she had hoped for. Feared. Wanted and dreaded in equal measure.

"Nathaniel..."

"I know I shouldn't say this. I know there are a hundred reasons why this is wrong. Why we can't..." He reached for her hand. "But I can't keep pretending. I can't keep acting like you're just another worker. Like my feelings don't exist."

Clara looked at their joined hands. She should pull away. She should tell him the truth. About who she was. About her father. About Thomas. About everything.

But the words wouldn't come. Instead, she said, "I care for you too."

Nathaniel's eyes widened. "You do?"

"Yes. I've tried not to. I've tried to keep my distance. But I can't help it."

Nathaniel moved closer. His free hand reached up. Almost touched her face. "Clara, I..."

The door opened behind them. A woman's voice called out. "Nathaniel? Are you out here?"

Nathaniel dropped Clara's hand and stepped back. Clara felt the loss of his touch like a physical pain.

An older woman appeared on the balcony. She wore an expensive gown and jewels. Her face was stern. Disapproving.

"There you are," the woman said. "Your father is looking for you. He wants to introduce you to someone."

"Of course." Nathaniel's voice was controlled. Polite. But Clara heard the frustration underneath. "I'll be there shortly."

The woman's eyes shifted to Clara. They were cold. Assessing. "Who is this?"

"A guest," Nathaniel said firmly.

"I see." The woman's tone suggested she saw quite a lot. None of it good. "Well, don't keep your father waiting."

She disappeared back inside.

Nathaniel turned to Clara. "I'm sorry. I have to..."

"I understand. Go."

"Will you wait for me?"

Clara shook her head. "I should go home. It's getting late."

"But..."

"Nathaniel, this was lovely. But we both know it can't go any further. There are too many complications. Too many secrets."

"What secrets?"

Clara looked away. "Mine. Yours. The factory's. All of them."

Nathaniel reached for her again but stopped himself. "Will I see you Monday? At the factory?"

"Yes."

"Good." Nathaniel hesitated. Then he said, "Tonight meant something to me. I hope it meant something to you too."

"It did."

"Then it's not over. Whatever this is between us. It's not finished."

Clara wanted to believe him. But she knew better. This moment on the balcony. This almost-confession. It was as close as they could ever come.

Because if Nathaniel knew the truth about her, everything would change. He would see her differently. Maybe hate her for the lies. For the deception.

And if Clara told him about Thomas, about his father, about the journal hidden in her shop, it would destroy him.

So she said nothing. She just nodded. Let him believe there could be more.

Nathaniel went back inside. Clara stood alone on the balcony. The cold bit through his jacket. But she didn't move.

She thought about the dance. About his hand on her waist. About the way he had looked at her.

She thought about his words. I've come to care for you. More than I should.

And she thought about her own secrets. Growing heavier. More dangerous. Every day.

Clara knew she couldn't keep this up much longer. The lies. The hiding. The pretending.

Something would have to give. Soon.

But for tonight, she allowed herself to remember. The music. The dance. The moment when Nathaniel had almost told her he loved her.

Even if it could never happen again. Even if it was all built on lies.

For tonight, it had been real.

And that would have to be enough.

Chapter Twelve

CLARA ARRIVED AT THE factory on Monday morning feeling uneasy. The winter gathering had been two days ago. She had spent Sunday at home with her father, trying to forget the way Nathaniel had looked at her on the balcony. Trying to ignore the feelings growing in her chest.

But unease followed her like a shadow.

She walked through the factory gates and noticed workers watching her. More than usual. They whispered to each other. Pointed.

Clara kept her head down and hurried to her room.

Inside, she closed the door and leaned against it. Something was wrong. She could feel it.

A knock made her jump. Mr. Pell entered without waiting for permission. His face was grave.

"Clara. We need to talk."

"What's happened?"

Mr. Pell closed the door carefully. He lowered his voice. "Basil has been asking questions about you. About where you came from. Who you are."

Clara's blood ran cold. "What kind of questions?"

"Everything. Your background. Your training. Your real name." Mr. Pell looked at her with concern. "He's been offering money to anyone who can find information. One of the lads took it. Went to your neighbourhood. Asked around."

"No." The word came out as a whisper.

"I'm sorry, Clara. I tried to warn you. But Basil was too quick. Too determined."

Clara sank onto her stool. "Does Nathaniel know?"

"Not yet. But he will. Everyone will." Mr. Pell hesitated. "There's more."

"What?"

"Basil has printed flyers. He's planning to distribute them at the factory outing this afternoon."

"What outing?"

"The elder Mr. Blackwood arranged it. A celebration for completing a large order. All workers are required to attend." Mr. Pell's expression was sympathetic. "Clara, whatever is on those flyers, it will be made public today. In front of everyone."

Clara felt sick. She stood and paced the small room. "I have to leave. Now. Before it happens."

"If you leave, it will look like you have something to hide."

"I do have something to hide."

"Then maybe it's time to stop hiding." Mr. Pell moved towards the door. "I don't know what secrets you're keeping. But I know you're a good person. A skilled worker. Whatever Basil reveals, hold your head high. Don't let him see you break."

Mr. Pell left. Clara stood alone. Her hands were shaking. Her mind raced.

She could run. Leave the factory. Disappear. But Basil would still spread whatever information he had found. And running would make her look guilty.

Or she could stay. Face whatever was coming. But the thought terrified her.

The morning dragged on. Clara tried to work but her hands would not cooperate. Every sound made her jump. Every footstep in the corridor felt like a threat.

At noon, a bell rang. The factory fell silent. Workers began moving towards the yard.

Clara stayed in her room. Maybe she could avoid the outing. Stay hidden until it was over.

But a knock came at her door. A supervisor she did not know.

"All workers must attend. Mr. Blackwood's orders."

Clara had no choice. She followed the supervisor out into the corridor. Down the stairs. Out into the yard.

The space was crowded. Hundreds of workers gathered in groups. Tables had been set up with food and drink. A makeshift platform stood at one end.

Clara stayed at the back. Near the factory wall. Where she might escape if needed.

Workers stared at her. Some smiled nastily. Others looked curious. A few seemed sympathetic.

Across the yard, Clara saw Nathaniel. He stood near the platform with his father and several managers. He was looking for someone. His eyes scanned the crowd.

When he saw Clara, his expression changed. Relief. Then concern. He started moving towards her.

But before he could reach her, Basil Thorn stepped onto the platform. He held a stack of papers in his hand. His voice carried across the yard.

"Good afternoon, everyone. I hope you're enjoying the celebration." Basil's smile was sharp. Predatory. "I have something interesting to share with you all. Something that concerns one of our workers."

The crowd quieted. All eyes turned to Basil.

"As you know, we pride ourselves on honesty at Blackwood and Sons. On transparency. On knowing who we employ." Basil held up one of the papers. "So imagine my surprise when I discovered that one of our workers has been lying to us. About who they are. What they are."

Clara's heart pounded. She wanted to run. But her feet would not move.

"Most of you have heard of C. Wren. The mysterious watchmaker whose repairs have been so praised by

Mr. Nathaniel Blackwood." Basil's voice dripped with mockery. "Well, I have discovered something fascinating about C. Wren."

He held up the paper so everyone could see. Large letters. Clear words.

C. WREN IS A GIRL.

The yard erupted. Gasps. Shouts. Laughter.

Clara felt every eye turn to her. Staring. Judging.

"That's right," Basil continued. "The talented C. Wren, who has been working in our factory under false pretences, is actually Clara Wren. A girl of eighteen. Daughter of a failed watchmaker. Who has been deceiving us all."

The words hit Clara like physical blows. Failed watchmaker. Deceiving.

Someone shouted from the crowd. "Women can't do watch repair!"

"It's indecent!" another voice called.

"She's been taking a man's job!"

Basil raised his hand for silence. "I believe Miss Wren owes us all an explanation. Miss Wren? Would you care to defend yourself?"

All eyes turned to Clara. Hundreds of faces. Some angry. Some disgusted. Some merely curious.

Clara opened her mouth. But no words came. What could she say? Basil was right. She had lied. Deceived them all.

"Nothing to say?" Basil's smile widened. "How disappointing."

"That's enough, Basil." Nathaniel pushed through the crowd. He climbed onto the platform. "This is not appropriate."

"Isn't it? I'm simply revealing the truth." Basil gestured to Clara. "Your special worker. Your talented artisan. She's been lying to you. To all of us. About who she is."

"Her identity doesn't change the quality of her work."

"Doesn't it? How do we know any of her work was genuine? Maybe her father did it. Maybe she just signed her name."

"I've seen her work. I know it's hers."

"You're defending her?" Basil's voice rose. "Even after she deceived you? Even after she made a fool of you?"

Nathaniel's face darkened. "I'm defending a skilled worker who has done good work for this factory. Her gender is irrelevant."

"Her gender is everything!" Basil turned to the crowd. "This is exactly the problem. Women thinking they can do men's work. Taking jobs from honest men who need to feed their families. It's wrong. It's unnatural."

The crowd murmured agreement. Clara felt tears burning in her eyes. She would not cry. She would not give them the satisfaction.

But the shame was overwhelming. The humiliation. She had been exposed. Revealed. Made into a spectacle.

Clara turned and ran. She pushed through the crowd. Workers stepped aside. Some jeered. Some laughed.

She ran through the factory. Up the stairs. To her room. She grabbed her shawl. Her few personal belongings.

Behind her, footsteps. "Clara, wait!"

Nathaniel stood in the doorway. Out of breath. His expression was anguished.

"Don't go. Please."

"I have to. You saw what happened out there. I can't stay."

"I'll talk to the board. Explain. They'll understand."

"Will they?" Clara faced him. "Basil was right. I lied. I deceived everyone. Including you."

"You did what you had to do. To survive. To work."

"It doesn't matter why I did it. What matters is that I'm not welcome here. I never was."

Nathaniel moved closer. "Clara, please. Give me time. I can fix this."

"You can't fix this. No one can." Clara pulled on her shawl. "Your father will demand I be dismissed. The board will agree. It's over."

"Then I'll resign. We'll start our own workshop. Together."

"Don't be foolish. You can't throw away your position for me."

"Why not?"

"Because..." Clara stopped. The truth sat on her tongue. Heavy. Dangerous. "Because I'm not worth it."

"You are. Clara, you're the most talented watch-maker I've ever met. Male or female. You're brilliant. And I..." Nathaniel reached for her hand. "I care about you. Deeply."

Clara pulled her hand away. "You care about some-one who doesn't really exist. Someone who's been ly-ing to you from the start."

"That's not true."

"It is. Everything about me has been a lie. My name. My position. All of it." Clara moved towards the door. "I need to go home. To my father. This is my fault. I should never have come here."

"Clara..."

She pushed past him. Ran down the stairs. Out of the factory. Into the street.

The cold air hit her face. The smoke from chimneys hung in the grey sky. Clara ran until her lungs burned. Until she could not run anymore.

Then she walked. Through the streets. Past shops and houses. People stared at her. A young woman alone. Crying. Running.

Clara did not care. The shame was too deep. The humiliation too complete.

She reached home and let herself in. The shop was quiet. Empty. Her father was upstairs. Sleeping probably.

Clara climbed the stairs slowly. Every step felt heavy. She knocked on her father's door.

"Come in."

Her father was sitting up in bed. He looked weak. Tired. But his eyes were alert.

"Clara? What's wrong? You're home early."

Clara sat on the edge of the bed. The tears came then. Hot and fast. She could not stop them.

"Oh, my dear girl." Her father pulled her close. "What happened?"

"They found out. At the factory. About who I am. What I am." Clara's voice broke. "They humiliated me. In front of everyone. Said I was a liar. A fraud."

Her father's arms tightened around her. "I'm sorry. I'm so sorry. This is my fault. I should have protected you better."

"It's not your fault. I chose to go there. I chose to lie."

"You did what you had to do. To survive. To keep us afloat." Her father's voice was fierce. "You have nothing to be ashamed of."

"Then why do I feel so ashamed?"

"Because the world is cruel to women who step outside their place. But that doesn't make you wrong. It makes them wrong."

Clara pulled back. Looked at her father. "I can't go back there. Ever."

"I know."

"So what do we do now?"

Her father was quiet for a long moment. Then he said, "We survive. The way we always have. You'll keep repairing watches here. In the shop. Under your own name. And anyone who doesn't like it can take their business elsewhere."

"No one will come. Not once word spreads."

"Then we'll find a way. Together." Her father squeezed her hand. "You're strong, Clara. Stronger than you know. You'll get through this."

Clara wanted to believe him. But the shame still burned. The humiliation still ached.

She had been exposed. Revealed. And nothing would ever be the same.

That evening, Clara sat in the workshop. The clocks ticked around her. Steady. Reliable. Uncaring.

She thought about the factory. About the crowd of faces. The jeers. The laughter.

She thought about Nathaniel. About the pain in his eyes when she ran. About his offer to resign. To start fresh.

But how could they start fresh? She was ruined. Her reputation destroyed. And Nathaniel would only destroy his own by associating with her.

Clara picked up a watch. One of her father's old repairs. She opened it. Looked at the mechanism inside.

This was what she knew. This was what she was good at. Not navigating the complicated world of factories and hierarchies. Not playing at being someone she was not.

She was a watchmaker. The daughter of a watchmaker. That was all she had ever been.

And maybe that was enough.

Clara closed the watch and set it aside. She stood and looked around the workshop. At the tools. The parts. The familiar space.

Tomorrow she would begin again. Here. In her father's shop. Under her own name. As herself.

It would be difficult. People would talk. Customers would stay away.

But she would survive. She always had.

Clara climbed the stairs to her room. She lay down on her bed and stared at the ceiling.

Her secret was out. Her lies exposed.

And she had never felt more alone.

Chapter Thirteen

TWO DAYS PASSED. CLARA did not leave the house. She could not face the streets. The stares. The whispers. Everyone in Birmingham would know by now. The girl who pretended to be a watchmaker. The fraud.

She spent the time in the workshop. Sorting tools. Cleaning parts. Doing anything to keep her hands busy. To stop her mind from replaying the humiliation at the factory.

Her father watched her with worried eyes. He said little. But his silence was heavy. Full of things unsaid.

On the third morning, Clara sat at the workbench. The journal lay in front of her. The one she had found weeks ago. The one with her father's entries about Thomas Blackwood.

She had read it again last night. Every word. Every date. The story it told.

Clara heard footsteps on the stairs. Her father appeared in the doorway. He was wrapped in a blanket despite the warmth from the small stove. He looked thin. Frail. But his eyes were clear.

"May I sit with you?" he asked.

"Of course, Papa."

Her father settled into the old chair by the window. The one he used to sit in when he worked. Before the illness took his strength.

He saw the journal on the bench. His expression changed. Became pained.

"You found it," he said quietly.

"Yes. Weeks ago. I'm sorry. I didn't mean to pry."

"Don't apologise. I should have told you years ago." Her father's hands trembled slightly. "I should have been honest with you. About everything."

Clara picked up the journal. "Tell me now. Please. I need to understand."

Her father was quiet for a long moment. Then he began to speak.

"Thomas Blackwood came to me fifteen years ago. He was young. Eager. He wanted to learn watchmaking. Not the factory way. The proper way. With care. With attention to detail."

"Why did he come to you?"

"His father wanted him to learn the business side. Management. Profit margins. But Thomas didn't care about any of that. He loved the craft. The precision. The beauty of a well-made watch." Her father's voice was soft. Remembering. "So he came to me. In secret. His father didn't know. Or if he did, he pretended not to."

Clara leaned forward. "What was he like?"

"Kind. Thoughtful. Brilliant, really. He had a gift for understanding how things worked. How they could be improved." Her father smiled sadly. "He reminded me of you. The same passion. The same dedication."

"You trained him for how long?"

"Two years. He came three times a week. Sometimes more. We worked on repairs together. I taught him everything I knew." Her father's expression darkened. "And then things changed."

"What happened?"

Her father sighed. "Thomas started noticing things. Patterns. Designs that appeared in Blackwood watches that he had never seen in the factory. Mechanisms that looked familiar."

"Your designs," Clara said.

"Yes. And others. Thomas began investigating. Quietly. He found letters. Payments made to factory workers. Instructions to copy designs from other watchmakers. To bring them back to the factory. To reproduce them as Blackwood originals."

Clara felt anger rising in her chest. "His father was stealing."

"Not just stealing. Destroying livelihoods. Small workshops like ours. We couldn't compete when our own designs were being mass produced and sold cheaper." Her father's voice was bitter. "Three of my best designs ended up in Blackwood watches. I lost customers. Lost income. I thought it was bad luck. Bad timing. I didn't realise it was theft."

"But Thomas found out."

"Yes. And he was horrified. He gathered evidence. Documents. Testimonies from workers who had been paid to steal. He wanted to expose his father. To make things right."

Clara thought about the journal entries. About Thomas's determination. "What did he do?"

"He came to me. Showed me everything he had found. Asked for my help. My testimony." Her father's voice cracked. "And I said no."

Clara stared at her father. "Why?"

"Because I was afraid. Afraid of what the elder Blackwood would do. Afraid of losing what little I had left. Afraid for you." Her father's hands covered his face. "I told Thomas it was too dangerous. That he should let it go. But he wouldn't listen."

"He tried to blow the whistle anyway."

"Yes. He went to the factory board. To inspectors. He tried to make them listen. To make them investigate." Her father lowered his hands. His eyes were wet. "And then he died."

Clara's throat felt tight. "The factory collapse."

"They said it was an accident. Poor maintenance. Rotten floorboards on the third level. Thomas fell three storeys. Died instantly." Her father's voice shook. "But I didn't believe it. I still don't."

"You think it was orchestrated."

"I don't know. I can't prove anything. But the timing... Thomas was about to go to the newspapers. About to make everything public. And then suddenly he's dead. The investigation closes quickly. The factory is repaired. Everything goes back to normal." Her father looked at Clara. "It was too convenient."

Clara felt cold. "Did you tell anyone? About your suspicions?"

"Who would I tell? The police? They were in the elder Blackwood's pocket. The inspectors? Same thing. I had no proof. Just a feeling. A terrible certainty that Thomas had been silenced."

"So you did nothing."

"I did nothing." Her father's shame was palpable. "I kept my head down. Protected what I had. Protected you. And I've lived with the guilt ever since."

Clara stood and paced the workshop. Her mind raced. Everything made sense now. Her father's warnings about the Blackwoods. His fear when she took the commission. His anger when she went to work at the factory.

"That's why you didn't want me near them," Clara said. "You were afraid the same thing would happen to me."

"Yes. I was terrified. When you told me about Nathaniel's letter, about the commission, I thought..." Her father's voice broke. "I thought I might lose you too."

Clara moved to her father's chair. She knelt beside him. "Papa, I'm sorry. I should have listened to you."

"No. You were right to take the work. Right to prove yourself. I was wrong to ask you to hide." Her father touched her face gently. "I've spent fifteen years hiding from the truth. From the guilt. From the fear. And all it did was make me smaller. Weaker. I won't let that happen to you."

"What do we do now?"

"Now?" Her father looked at the journal on the bench. "Now we tell the truth. All of it. About the stolen designs. About Thomas. About what really happened."

Clara felt a surge of determination. "We could go to the newspapers. Show them the journal. Your testimony."

"It might not be enough. My journal is just one man's suspicions. We need more."

"Then we'll find more. There must be records. Old workers who remember. Someone who knows the truth about the collapse."

Her father studied her face. "Clara, this is dangerous. If the elder Blackwood really did orchestrate Thomas's death, he won't hesitate to come after us. After you."

"I don't care. Thomas deserves justice. You deserve justice." Clara's voice was fierce. "And I won't let fear stop me. Not anymore."

Her father was quiet. Then he said, "You're braver than I ever was."

"No. I'm just tired of hiding. Tired of being ashamed." Clara stood. "We've lost everything already. Our reputation. Our income. What more can they take from us?"

"Our lives."

"Then we'll be careful. But we won't be silent."
Clara picked up the journal. "Thomas tried to expose
the truth. He died for it. The least we can do is finish
what he started."

Her father nodded slowly. "All right. But we do this
smart. We gather evidence first. Build a case. Make it
impossible for them to deny."

"Where do we start?"

"The factory collapse. There would have been an
official investigation. Reports. Witness statements. If
we can find those records, we might find inconsisten-
cies. Things that don't add up."

"And the workers who were paid to steal designs.
Some of them must still be alive. Still in Birmingham."

"Maybe. But they'll be afraid to talk. The elder
Blackwood has a long memory. And a long reach."

Clara thought about Nathaniel. About his kindness. His integrity. About the pain in his eyes when he
talked about Thomas.

"What about Nathaniel?" she asked quietly.

Her father's expression grew troubled. "What about
him?"

"He loved his brother. He's been grieving for three years. If we tell him the truth, if we show him the evidence..."

"He might not believe us. Or worse, he might believe us and side with his father anyway. Blood is thick, Clara. Family loyalty can be stronger than truth."

"But it might not be. Nathaniel is different from his father. He cares about doing the right thing. About honesty."

"How well do you really know him? You worked at the factory for a few weeks. You shared a dance at a gathering. That's not enough to know someone's character."

Clara thought about Nathaniel's defence of her at the factory outing. About his offer to resign. About the way he had looked at her on the balcony.

"I know him well enough," she said.

Her father sighed. "Clara, I understand you have feelings for him. But this is bigger than feelings. This is about survival. About justice. We can't trust a Blackwood. Not even Nathaniel."

"But he deserves to know the truth. About his brother. About his father."

"Maybe. But not yet. Not until we have solid proof. Something undeniable." Her father reached for her hand. "Promise me you'll be careful. That you won't go to him until we have everything we need."

Clara hesitated. Then she nodded. "I promise."

But even as she said it, she knew it would be difficult. Nathaniel had tried to help her. Had defended her. She owed him the truth.

But her father was right. They needed proof first. Real evidence. Something that couldn't be dismissed or explained away.

"So where do we start?" Clara asked. "How do we find the collapse records?"

"The Birmingham city archives. They keep records of all official investigations. Industrial accidents. Deaths. If the reports exist, they'll be there."

"I'll go tomorrow."

"We'll go together."

"Papa, you're not strong enough."

"I'm strong enough for this." Her father's voice was firm. "Thomas died because I was too afraid to help him. I won't make that mistake again."

Clara squeezed his hand. "All right. We'll go together."

They sat in silence for a moment. The workshop around them was quiet except for the ticking of clocks. The familiar sound that had filled Clara's whole life.

"Papa?" Clara said quietly. "Do you think we can win? Against the Blackwoods?"

Her father was quiet for a long time. Then he said, "I don't know. They have money. Power. Influence. We have nothing but the truth."

"Is that enough?"

"Sometimes. Not always. But it's all we have." Her father looked at her. "The question isn't whether we can win. It's whether we can live with ourselves if we don't try."

Clara understood. This wasn't about winning. It wasn't even about revenge. It was about honouring Thomas's memory. About clearing her father's name. About standing up for what was right.

Even if it cost them everything.

"Then we try," Clara said.

"Then we try," her father agreed.

Clara picked up the journal and held it close. This small book contained the seeds of everything. The stolen designs. The suspicions about Thomas's death. The guilt and fear that had consumed her father for fifteen years.

Now it would be their weapon. Their proof. Their way of fighting back.

But first they needed more. More evidence. More testimony. More truth.

Clara looked at her father. He looked tired. Frail. But there was something in his eyes she hadn't seen in years. Determination. Purpose. Hope.

"We should rest tonight," Clara said. "Tomorrow we'll go to the archives. Start searching."

"Yes. Tomorrow." Her father stood slowly. Clara helped him. "Clara?"

"Yes?"

"I'm proud of you. Whatever happens, I want you to know that. I'm proud of your courage. Your skill. Your heart."

Clara felt tears prick her eyes. "Thank you, Papa."

Her father kissed her forehead. Then he shuffled towards the door. At the threshold, he paused.

"One more thing," he said. "Don't underestimate the Blackwoods. Not the father. Not Basil. Not even Nathaniel. They're dangerous people. All of them."

"I'll be careful."

"See that you are."

Her father disappeared up the stairs. Clara heard his slow footsteps. The creak of his bedroom door.

She sat alone in the workshop. The journal in her hands. The weight of what they were about to do settling on her shoulders.

They were going to take on the most powerful family in Birmingham. With nothing but an old journal and determination.

It seemed impossible. Foolish. Dangerous.

But Clara thought about Thomas. About the young man who had come to this workshop. Who had learned the craft. Who had tried to do the right thing.

And she thought about Nathaniel. About his grief. About his right to know the truth.

Whatever happened, they would not stop. They would not give up. They would see this through.

For Thomas. For her father. For justice.

Clara set the journal down carefully. Tomorrow they would begin. Tomorrow they would start fighting back.

Tonight, she would rest. And prepare. And gather her courage.

Because the battle ahead would not be easy. And they would need every ounce of strength they could muster.

Chapter Fourteen

C LARA AND HER FATHER spent three days searching the city archives. They found the official report on the factory collapse. It was brief. Vague. It blamed poor maintenance and rotten floor-boards. No one was held responsible.

But the report also mentioned the name of the inspector who had investigated. Inspector Hadley. Retired now. Living somewhere in Birmingham.

It took Clara another two days to find his address. A small house on the edge of the city. Modest. Quiet.

She went alone. Her father was too weak for the journey. He had argued. But Clara insisted. If Inspector Hadley was nervous about talking, one person would be less threatening than two.

Clara stood outside the house and took a deep breath. Then she knocked.

An old man answered. He was tall but stooped. Grey hair. Weathered face. Sharp eyes that studied Clara carefully.

"Yes?"

"Inspector Hadley?"

"I haven't been an inspector for three years. Just Hadley now." His voice was gruff. "What do you want?"

"My name is Clara Wren. I wanted to ask you about an investigation. From three years ago. The factory collapse at Blackwood and Sons."

Hadley's expression changed. Became guarded. "I don't talk about old cases."

"Please. It's important. My father knew Thomas Blackwood. The man who died. We think there's more to the story than the official report says."

"The report says everything that needs to be said."

"Does it?" Clara met his eyes. "Or does it say what someone wanted it to say?"

Hadley was quiet for a long moment. Then he said, "You should go."

"Please. Just five minutes. That's all I'm asking."

"Why? What good will it do? It's been three years. The case is closed."

"Because Thomas deserves the truth. And so does his brother."

At the mention of Nathaniel, Hadley's expression shifted again. "Nathaniel Blackwood sent you?"

"No. But I know him. I've worked at the factory. And I know he's been grieving for three years. Wondering what really happened to his brother."

Hadley studied her face. Then he sighed. "Come in. But I can only give you five minutes."

Clara followed him inside. The house was small but tidy. Books lined the walls. A fire burned in the grate.

Hadley gestured to a chair. Clara sat. He remained standing.

"What do you want to know?" he asked.

"The truth. About what happened that day. About the collapse."

"The truth is in the report."

"Is it? Or is that just what you were told to write?"

Hadley's jaw tightened. "Be very careful with your accusations, Miss Wren."

"I'm not accusing you. I'm asking for your help." Clara leaned forward. "Thomas Blackwood was investigating his father. He found evidence of stolen designs. Of fraud. He was about to expose it all. And then he died. Don't you think that's suspicious?"

"Suspicious doesn't mean criminal."

"But you had doubts. Didn't you?"

Hadley was quiet. Then he moved to the window. Looked out at the street. "Yes. I had doubts."

Clara's heart raced. "What kind of doubts?"

"The floorboards were rotten. That part was true. But they shouldn't have given way under Thomas's weight. Not completely. Not catastrophically." Hadley turned to face her. "I examined the beams. The supports. Some of them looked tampered with. Weakened deliberately."

"Did you put that in your report?"

"I tried. My supervisor removed it. Said I was speculating. That I had no proof."

"But you did have proof."

"I had observations. Suspicions. Not proof."
Hadley's voice was bitter. "And when I pushed, I was
told to close the case. Move on. Stop causing trouble."

"Who told you that?"

"People with power. People who didn't want questions asked." Hadley moved to a cabinet. He opened
a drawer and pulled out a small leather-bound book.
"Thomas Blackwood came to see me. Two weeks before he died. He wanted to give me this. For safekeeping, he said."

Clara stared at the book. "What is it?"

"A ledger. Names. Dates. Payments made to factory workers. Instructions to steal designs from other
workshops. All in Thomas's handwriting. With documents attached. Letters. Receipts. Proof."

"Why didn't you use it? Why didn't you investigate?"

"Because Thomas died before I could. And after his
death, I was warned. Very clearly. Very directly. If I
pursued the matter, I would lose my position. Maybe
worse." Hadley looked at the ledger. "I kept it. All these
years. I told myself I was waiting for the right moment.
But really, I was just afraid."

"Can I see it?"

Hadley hesitated. Then he handed her the ledger. "If you use this, you'll make enemies. Powerful enemies. The Blackwoods have reach. Influence. They'll come after you."

"They already have." Clara opened the ledger. Her hands trembled. Inside were pages of neat handwriting. Thomas's handwriting. Lists of names. Dates. Amounts paid. And tucked between the pages, documents. Letters from the elder Blackwood. Instructions to factory foremen. Evidence of systematic theft.

Clara's breath caught. "This is it. This proves everything."

"Yes. But be careful how you use it. The elder Blackwood is ruthless. If he thinks you're a threat, he won't hesitate to destroy you."

"I understand." Clara closed the ledger and held it carefully. "Thank you. For keeping this. For trusting me with it."

"Don't thank me. I should have done something three years ago. I should have stood up to them." Hadley's voice was heavy with regret. "But I was afraid. And Thomas died because of my cowardice."

"You weren't a coward. You were outmatched. Alone." Clara stood. "But you're helping now. And that matters."

Hadley walked her to the door. "Miss Wren? One more thing. Be careful who you trust. Even within the Blackwood family. Not everyone is who they seem."

Clara thought about Nathaniel. About his kindness. His integrity. "I'll be careful."

She left the house with the ledger tucked under her arm. Her heart pounded. This was it. The proof they needed. The evidence that could bring down the elder Blackwood.

But first, she had to tell Nathaniel. He deserved to know the truth about his brother. About his father. About everything.

Clara walked through the streets towards Nathaniel's home. He had given her his address weeks ago. She had never used it. But now she had no choice.

The house was large. Elegant. Everything the Wren shop was not. Clara stood outside and almost turned back. Then she thought about Thomas. About the truth he had died trying to reveal.

She knocked.

A servant answered. "Yes?"

"I need to see Nathaniel Blackwood. It's urgent."

"Mr. Blackwood is not receiving visitors."

"Please. Tell him Clara Wren is here. He'll want to see me."

The servant looked doubtful. But he disappeared inside. A few minutes later, Nathaniel appeared. He looked tired. Drawn. But when he saw Clara, his expression changed to surprise. Then relief.

"Clara. I've been trying to find you. To see if you were all right. After what happened at the factory..."

"I'm fine. But I need to speak with you. Privately."

Nathaniel glanced at the servant. "We'll talk in the study. Follow me."

He led Clara through elegant corridors to a small room lined with books. He closed the door behind them.

"What's happened? Is your father well?"

"My father is fine. But there's something I need to tell you. About Thomas. About your father. About everything." Clara held up the ledger. "I found proof. Of what really happened. Of why Thomas died."

Nathaniel stared at the ledger. "What is that?"

"Thomas kept records. Of the stolen designs. The payments. All of it. He gave this to Inspector Hadley two weeks before he died. For safekeeping."

"How did you get it?"

"I went to see Hadley. Asked him about the collapse. He gave me this." Clara handed the ledger to Nathaniel. "You need to read it. All of it."

Nathaniel opened the ledger. His face was pale. He read silently. Page after page. Document after document.

Clara watched him. Saw the shock. The pain. The anger.

Finally, Nathaniel looked up. His eyes were wet. "My father did this. He stole from other watchmakers. Destroyed their livelihoods. And Thomas tried to stop him."

"Yes."

"And the collapse. It wasn't an accident, was it?"

Clara told him everything. About her father training Thomas. About the journal. About Hadley's suspicions. About the weakened supports.

When she finished, Nathaniel sat down heavily. He looked broken. "My father killed him. Maybe not with his own hands. But he arranged it. Had it done."

"We don't have absolute proof of that. Just suspicions. But the ledger proves the theft. The fraud. That's enough to ruin him."

"Why are you telling me this? Why not go to the newspapers? Expose everything?"

Clara sat beside him. "Because you deserve to know the truth first. About Thomas. About what he was fighting for. About why he died."

"You're giving me a choice. Whether to help you or protect my father."

"Yes."

Nathaniel was quiet for a long time. Then he said, "Thomas was the best of us. He cared about honour. About doing the right thing. And my father destroyed him for it." He looked at Clara. "I won't protect that. I won't be part of it anymore."

"What will you do?"

"Help you. Expose the truth. Get this ledger to the newspapers. Make sure everyone knows what Thomas was trying to do." Nathaniel's voice was firm. Resolved. "My father will retaliate. He'll try to destroy you. Me. Anyone who stands against him."

"I know."

"And you're still willing to do this?"

"Yes. For Thomas. For my father. For everyone the elder Blackwood has hurt."

Nathaniel took her hand. "Then we'll do it together. Quietly. Carefully. We'll get the ledger to a journalist we can trust. Someone who can't be bought or threatened."

"Do you know someone like that?"

"I think so. A man named Pritchard. He writes for the Birmingham Gazette. He's been critical of factory owners before. Of the conditions. The corruption. He'll listen."

"When?"

"Tomorrow. I'll arrange a meeting. Bring the ledger. We'll show him everything."

Clara nodded. Relief washed over her. She was not alone in this anymore. Nathaniel was with her. Fighting beside her.

"Thank you," she said quietly. "For believing me. For standing with me."

"I should be thanking you. For finding the truth. For giving me a chance to honour Thomas's memory." Nathaniel squeezed her hand. "Clara, I'm sorry. For everything that happened at the factory. For not stopping Basil. For not protecting you better."

"It wasn't your fault."

"It feels like it was."

They sat in silence. The study was warm. Quiet. Outside, the city sounds were muffled. Distant.

Nathaniel still held Clara's hand. She became aware of how close they were sitting. How his thumb moved gently across her knuckles.

"Clara," Nathaniel said softly. "There's something I need to tell you."

"What?"

"When you ran from the factory. When I couldn't find you. I was terrified. I thought I'd lost you. That I'd never see you again." His voice was low. Intense. "And I realised something. I care about you. More than I should. More than is appropriate or reasonable."

Clara's breath caught. "Nathaniel..."

"I know this is complicated. Dangerous, even. My father will see you as an enemy. An upstart. Someone trying to destroy our family. But I don't care." Nathaniel turned to face her fully. "I've never met anyone like you. Your courage. Your skill. Your determination to do what's right no matter the cost. You inspire me. You make me want to be better. Braver."

"You're already brave."

"Not like you. But I'm trying. Because of you." Nathaniel lifted her hand. Pressed it to his chest. "I know I have no right to say this. Not now. Not when everything is so uncertain. But I need you to know. I love you, Clara. I think I've loved you since the moment you argued with me about watch designs. Since you looked at me like I was an equal. Not a title. Not a name. Just a person."

Clara felt tears in her eyes. "I love you too."

The words came out before she could stop them. But they were true. She had fought against the feeling for weeks. Tried to deny it. But sitting here with Nathaniel. With the truth finally spoken. With the future so uncertain and dangerous. She could not lie anymore.

"You do?"

"Yes. I've tried not to. I've told myself it was impossible. That our worlds were too different. That your father would never allow it. But I can't help it. I love you."

Nathaniel's hand cupped her face. Gentle. Reverent. "Then we have something worth fighting for. Not just justice for Thomas. Not just exposing the truth. But a future. Together."

"If we survive."

"We'll survive. We have to." Nathaniel's thumb traced her cheek. "Because I'm not ready to lose you. Not now. Not ever."

He leaned closer. Clara's heart raced. She knew what was coming. What they were about to cross.

Nathaniel's lips touched hers. Soft. Hesitant. Asking permission.

Clara kissed him back. Her hand moved to his neck. Pulled him closer.

The kiss deepened. Became less hesitant. More certain. Electric.

When they finally pulled apart, both were breathless.

"I've wanted to do that for weeks," Nathaniel said.

"So have I."

They sat close. Foreheads touching. Hands entwined.

Outside, the world continued. But in this moment, in this room, nothing else mattered.

They had the truth. They had each other. And they had a plan.

Tomorrow they would meet with Pritchard. Show him the ledger. Start the process of exposing the elder Blackwood.

It would be dangerous. Difficult. The elder Blackwood would fight back. He would use every tool at his disposal to destroy them.

But Clara and Nathaniel would stand together. United. Fighting for justice. For Thomas. For the future they wanted to build.

And maybe, just maybe, they would win.

Clara pulled back slightly. Looked into Nathaniel's eyes. "What happens next?"

"We fight. We expose the truth. We face whatever comes." Nathaniel smiled. "Together."

"Together," Clara agreed.

They stood. Nathaniel walked her to the door. At the threshold, he kissed her once more. Brief. Tender.

"Be careful going home. The streets aren't safe at night."

"I will."

"I'll send word tomorrow. About the meeting with Pritchard."

"I'll be ready."

Clara left the house. The ledger was still tucked under her arm. The proof of everything. The weapon they would use against the elder Blackwood.

But more than that, she left with hope. With love. With the knowledge that she was not fighting alone anymore.

Nathaniel was with her. And together, they were stronger.

Clara walked through the dark streets towards home. The shops were closed. The lamps lit. Smoke hung in the air.

But for the first time in weeks, Clara felt light. Determined. Ready.

Tomorrow they would begin the real battle. The dangerous one.

But tonight, she allowed herself to feel happy. To re-member Nathaniel's kiss. To believe in the possibility of a future together.

Whatever came next, they would face it. Side by side.

And that made all the difference.

Chapter Fifteen

The meeting with Pritchard had been arranged for the following afternoon. But news travelled fast in Birmingham. Especially news about the Blackwoods.

Someone had talked. Or someone had seen Clara entering Nathaniel's house. Or perhaps Basil had been watching. Waiting.

However it happened, the elder Blackwood knew.

Clara arrived at the factory at noon. Nathaniel had sent word asking her to meet him there. They would go together to see Pritchard. Present a united front.

Clara walked through the factory gates. Workers stared at her. Some whispered. The girl who had been exposed. The fraud. What was she doing back here?

Clara kept her head high. She had nothing to be ashamed of anymore. The truth was coming out. Finally.

She climbed the stairs to Nathaniel's office. The door was closed. She could hear voices inside. Raised voices. Angry.

Clara knocked. The voices stopped abruptly.

"Come in," Nathaniel called.

Clara opened the door. Nathaniel stood by his desk. His face was pale. Tense.

And across from him stood his father.

Archibald Blackwood was exactly as Clara had imagined. Tall. Imposing. Steel-grey hair and beard. Cold eyes that assessed her immediately. Dismissed her just as quickly.

"So this is the girl," the elder Blackwood said. His voice was deep. Commanding. "The one causing all this trouble."

"Father, this is Clara Wren. Clara, my father."

Clara did not curtsy. Did not bow her head. She met the elder Blackwood's gaze directly. "Mr. Blackwood."

"Miss Wren." The elder Blackwood turned back to his son. "Wait in the corridor, girl. This conversation doesn't concern you."

"Yes, it does," Nathaniel said firmly. "Clara is with me. We're working together."

"Working together?" The elder Blackwood's laugh was harsh. "Is that what you call it? You've taken up with a girl who lied her way into my factory. Who has been spreading vicious rumours about our family. And now you claim you're working together?"

"The rumours aren't rumours. They're facts." Nathaniel moved to stand beside Clara. "Thomas kept records. Evidence. Of the stolen designs. The payments made to workers. All of it."

The elder Blackwood's expression darkened. "Thomas is dead. His wild accusations died with him."

"No, they didn't." Clara spoke up. Her voice was steady. Strong. "Thomas kept the evidence and gave it to someone. For safekeeping. I have it now. And we're taking it to the newspapers."

The elder Blackwood's eyes fixed on Clara. They were hard. Dangerous. "You're making a very serious accusation, Miss Wren. Without proof, that's slander. And slander has consequences."

"I have proof. A ledger. In Thomas's own handwriting. With documents attached. Letters you wrote. Instructions you gave. Everything."

"Show me."

"No."

The elder Blackwood's jaw tightened. "Then you're lying. If this ledger exists, show it to me."

"So you can destroy it? I don't think so." Clara took a step forward. "You stole my father's designs. You ruined his shop. His reputation. You built your fortune on the backs of honest craftsmen. And when Thomas tried to expose you, you had him killed."

The words hung in the air. Dangerous. Explosive.

The elder Blackwood's face went white with fury. "How dare you. How dare you accuse me of murder. You little upstart. You know nothing."

"I know that Thomas died two weeks before he was going to the newspapers. I know the factory collapse was suspicious. I know Inspector Hadley had doubts about the official report." Clara's voice rose. "And I know you're afraid. Because if the truth comes out, you'll lose everything."

"The only thing I'll lose is my patience." The elder Blackwood turned to Nathaniel. "Is this what you want? To side with this girl against your own father? Against your family?"

"I'm siding with the truth. Thomas tried to do the right thing. You destroyed him for it. I won't let that happen again."

"You're a fool. Both of you." The elder Blackwood moved towards the door. Then he stopped. Turned back. "Let me make something very clear. If you take this to the newspapers, there will be consequences. Legal consequences."

"We're not afraid of your lawyers," Clara said.

"You should be. I have evidence that your father signed a contract years ago. A non-disclosure agreement. Anything he knows about Blackwood business practices is confidential. If he talks, I'll sue him for breach of contract. I'll take his shop. His home. Everything."

Clara's stomach dropped. "You're lying."

"Am I? Ask him. Ask your father about the contract he signed after Thomas's death. When he was afraid. When he thought silence would protect him." The elder Blackwood's smile was cold. "I made sure he understood the terms very clearly."

Clara felt sick. Her father had never mentioned a contract. But it made sense. The fear. The guilt. The warnings.

"That contract was signed under duress," Nathaniel said. "It won't hold up."

"Perhaps. Perhaps not. Do you want to risk it?" The elder Blackwood looked at Clara. "Your father is ill. Dying, from what I hear. Do you really want to spend his last days fighting a legal battle he can't win?"

"You're a monster," Clara whispered.

"I'm a businessman. I protect what's mine. And I don't let anyone threaten my family's reputation. Not Thomas. Not you. Not even my own son."

The elder Blackwood turned his attention back to Nathaniel. "I'm giving you one chance. Walk away from this girl. Forget about the ledger. Go back to work. And I'll forget this moment of foolishness ever happened."

"No."

"Think carefully. If you defy me, you're cut off. No position at the factory. No inheritance. No access to family funds. You'll be on your own. Is she really worth that?"

Nathaniel didn't hesitate. "Yes."

The elder Blackwood's face twisted with rage. "Then you're no son of mine."

"I haven't been your son for a long time. Maybe never." Nathaniel's voice was calm but firm. "You killed Thomas. Maybe not with your own hands. But you orchestrated it. And I won't protect you anymore. I won't be part of this family's corruption."

"You'll regret this."

"The only thing I regret is not standing up to you sooner."

The elder Blackwood moved towards the door. "You have until the end of the day to clear out your office. After that, you're trespassing on my property."

He stopped at the threshold. Looked at Clara one more time. "And you, Miss Wren. Stay away from my factory. Stay away from my son. If I see you here again, I'll have you arrested for trespassing. And I'll make sure everyone in Birmingham knows exactly what kind of person you are. A liar. A fraud. A girl who seduced my son for money and revenge."

Clara's face burned. But she held his gaze. "Everyone will know what kind of person you are too. A thief. A killer. A man who destroyed his own son rather than admit the truth."

The elder Blackwood's expression was murderous. For a moment, Clara thought he might strike her. But he simply turned and walked out. The door slammed behind him.

The silence that followed was heavy. Oppressive.

Clara sank into a chair. Her legs felt weak. Her hands shook.

"I'm sorry," Nathaniel said quietly. "I knew he would be angry. But I didn't think..."

"He threatened my father. He threatened to take everything."

"The contract might not be real. He could be bluffing."

"Or he could be telling the truth." Clara looked up at Nathaniel. "I need to go home. I need to talk to my father. Find out if he signed something."

"I'll come with you."

"No. You need to pack your office. Get your things before he changes his mind and has you thrown out."

"Clara..."

"Please. I need to do this alone."

Nathaniel nodded reluctantly. "All right. But we still need to see Pritchard. This afternoon. Even if there's a contract, we can still expose the truth."

"What if your father sues? What if we lose everything?"

"Then we lose. But at least we'll have tried. At least we'll have told the truth." Nathaniel took her hands. "I meant what I said. You're worth it. All of it. The inheritance. The position. Even if it means starting over with nothing."

Clara felt tears sting her eyes. "You shouldn't have to choose."

"I'm not choosing. I already chose. The moment I read Thomas's ledger. The moment I understood what my father really is." Nathaniel pulled her close. "We'll get through this. Together."

Clara held onto him. Drew strength from his certainty. His courage.

"I love you," she whispered.

"I love you too."

They stood there for a long moment. Then Clara pulled away. "I have to go. I'll meet you at Pritchard's office. Three o'clock."

"I'll be there."

Clara left the factory. Workers watched her go. Some sneered. Some looked sympathetic. Most just looked confused.

Clara walked quickly through the streets. Her mind raced. A contract. A legal threat. Her father's illness.

Everything was falling apart. Just when they thought they had a chance. Just when they thought they could win.

Clara reached home. She burst through the door. Her father was in the workshop. He looked up, startled.

"Clara? What's wrong?"

"Did you sign a contract? With Archibald Blackwood? After Thomas died?"

Her father's face went pale. "How did you know about that?"

"He told me. Threatened me with it. Said if we go public with the truth, he'll sue you for breach of contract. Take everything we have."

Her father sank into his chair. "I'm sorry. I should have told you. But I was ashamed. Afraid."

"What does it say? The contract?"

"That I wouldn't speak about anything Thomas told me. About the factory. The stolen designs. Any of it. If I broke the agreement, I'd be liable for damages." Her father's voice was heavy. "He came to me right after Thomas died. Said he knew Thomas had been working with me. That I had information that could damage the family. He offered me money to stay quiet. A lot of money."

"Did you take it?"

"No. But I signed the contract anyway. Because he said if I didn't, he'd find a way to destroy what was left of my shop. My reputation. Everything." Her father looked at Clara with anguished eyes. "I was weak. I chose safety over truth. And I've regretted it every day since."

Clara knelt beside him. "It's not your fault. He manipulated you. Threatened you."

"But I gave in. I let him win. And now he's using it against you."

"We won't let him win this time." Clara took her father's hands. "We're still going to the newspapers. We're still exposing the truth. If he sues, we'll fight it."

"Clara, we can't afford a legal battle. We have nothing. No money. No resources."

"We have the truth. And we have people who will support us. Nathaniel. Inspector Hadley. Maybe others." Clara's voice was determined. "I won't let fear stop me. Not anymore."

Her father studied her face. Then he smiled. Sad but proud. "You're braver than I ever was."

"I learned from you. You taught me everything that matters. Skill. Integrity. Pride in my work." Clara squeezed his hands. "Now I'm going to use those lessons. To fight for what's right."

"Then I'm with you. Whatever happens, I'm with you."

Clara hugged him. Drew strength from him. Then she stood. "I have to go. We're meeting with a journalist. This afternoon. We're giving him the ledger."

"Be careful. The elder Blackwood is dangerous."

"I know. But so are we."

Clara left the house. The afternoon sun was hidden behind grey clouds. The streets were busy. People going about their lives. Unaware of the battle being fought in the shadows.

Clara walked to Pritchard's office. It was in a building near the city centre. Small. Cramped. But respectable.

Nathaniel was already there. Waiting outside. He looked tired. Worried. But when he saw Clara, his expression softened.

"How is your father?"

"The contract is real. But we're not backing down."

"Good." Nathaniel took her hand. "Are you ready?"

"Yes."

They went inside. A clerk led them to Pritchard's office. The journalist was older than Clara expected. Fifties, perhaps. Balding. Glasses perched on his nose. But his eyes were sharp. Intelligent.

"Mr Blackwood. And you must be Miss Wren." Pritchard gestured to chairs. "Sit. Please. Your message said you had information about Blackwood and Sons. Something important."

Nathaniel pulled out Thomas's ledger. He set it on Pritchard's desk. "This belonged to my brother, Thomas. He died three years ago in a factory collapse. But before he died, he was investigating our father. For fraud. For stealing designs from other watchmakers."

Pritchard opened the ledger. His eyebrows rose. "These are detailed records. Names. Dates. Amounts."

"Everything you need to prove systematic theft. My father built his fortune on stolen work. He ruined honest craftsmen. Destroyed their livelihoods." Nathaniel's voice was steady. "Thomas tried to expose him. And I believe my father had him killed to keep him quiet."

Pritchard looked up sharply. "That's a serious accusation."

"I know. We don't have absolute proof of murder. But the timing is suspicious. Thomas was about to go public. Two weeks later, he's dead in a convenient accident." Nathaniel gestured to the ledger. "But the theft is documented. Proven. That alone should be enough to bring him down."

Pritchard studied them both. "Why are you doing this? You're his son. This will destroy your family's reputation. Your inheritance. Everything."

"Because it's right. Because Thomas deserves justice. Because the people my father hurt deserve to have the truth told."

Pritchard turned to Clara. "And you? What's your stake in this?"

"My father was one of the people he stole from. He trained Thomas. Trusted him. And when Thomas died, he was threatened into silence." Clara's voice was calm. Clear. "I'm here to make sure the truth comes out. Whatever the cost."

Pritchard was quiet for a long moment. Then he said, "If I publish this, there will be lawsuits. Threats. The elder Blackwood has powerful friends. Connections."

"Will you publish it anyway?" Nathaniel asked.

Pritchard smiled. "I've been waiting for something like this for years. The Blackwoods have operated with impunity for too long. Someone needs to hold them accountable." He closed the ledger carefully. "I'll need time to verify everything. Check the records. Speak to some of the people named here. But if it all checks out, I'll run the story. Front page."

"How long?" Clara asked.

"A week. Maybe less."

"We can wait a week," Nathaniel said.

They left Pritchard's office. The ledger was in his hands now. The evidence. The truth. Soon it would be public knowledge.

Nathaniel and Clara walked together through the streets. Side by side. Partners.

"What happens now?" Clara asked.

"Now we prepare. My father will fight back. Hard. We need to be ready."

"Are you afraid?"

"Terrified. But also relieved." Nathaniel looked at her. "For the first time in three years, I feel like I'm doing something right. Honouring Thomas. Standing up for what matters."

"We'll face whatever comes. Together."

"Together," Nathaniel agreed.

They stopped outside Clara's shop. The building looked small. Shabby. But it was home.

"I should go in. My father will be worried."

"Clara?" Nathaniel took both her hands. "Thank you. For finding the truth. For pushing me to do this. For being brave when I was too afraid."

"You're not afraid anymore."

"No. Because of you."

He kissed her. Brief. Tender. A promise.

Then he walked away. Back towards his uncertain future.

Clara watched him go. Then she went inside. Her father was waiting.

"How did it go?"

"Pritchard will publish the story. Within a week."

Her father nodded. "Then it's done."

"Almost. We still have to wait. Prepare for whatever the elder Blackwood does next."

"We'll face it. Together."

Clara sat beside him. The workshop was quiet. Familiar. Safe.

But the battle was just beginning. And Clara knew that the coming days would be the hardest yet.

Still, for the first time, she felt hope. Real hope.

The truth was coming out. Justice for Thomas was within reach. And she and Nathaniel were together. Fighting side by side.

Whatever happened next, they would face it. Together.

And that made all the difference.

Chapter Sixteen

T WO DAYS AFTER THEY gave the ledger to
Pritchard, Clara and Nathaniel stood outside a
small shop on a quiet street. The building was narrow.
Two storeys. The ground floor had a large window
facing the street. The paint was peeling. The door
needed repair. But the structure was sound.

"What do you think?" Nathaniel asked.

Clara looked through the window. The space inside was empty. Dusty. But she could see the potential. A workshop at the back. A display area at
the front. Room for benches. Tools. Everything they
would need.

"It's perfect," she said.

"The rent is reasonable. And the landlord doesn't care who we are or what people say about us." Nathaniel pulled out a key. "Shall we look inside?"

They entered. The floorboards creaked under their feet. The air smelled of dust and old wood. Sunlight streamed through the dirty window, illuminating particles floating in the air.

Clara walked through the space. It was smaller than the Wren shop. But it felt full of promise. Full of possibility.

"We can work here," she said. "Make it into something good."

"We'll need to clean it. Repair some things. But yes. We can make it work." Nathaniel moved to stand beside her. "How much money do you have? For your share of the rent and supplies?"

Clara had counted her savings carefully. The coins hidden under the floorboard. The payment from her work at the factory. It was not much. But it was enough. "Twenty-three pounds."

"I have forty. From my personal accounts. My father froze access to the family funds. But I kept a separate account. For emergencies." Nathaniel looked around the shop. "Sixty-three pounds. It's not a fortune. But it's a start."

"We'll make it work. We have to."

They signed the lease that afternoon. The landlord barely looked at them. He just wanted the first month's rent. Clara and Nathaniel paid it together. Pooling their money. Becoming partners in every sense.

The next day, Clara returned with her father's tools. Box after box. She carried them carefully from the Wren shop to the new workshop. Her father helped as much as he could. But he was weak. Tired. Clara did most of the work herself.

Nathaniel arrived with tools of his own. Things he had bought over the years. Personal items. Not factory property.

They spent the day arranging the workshop. Setting up benches. Organizing tools. Clara's hands moved with practiced ease. Placing everything exactly where it needed to be.

"You're very particular about this," Nathaniel observed.

"Tools need to be accessible. Within reach. If you have to search for something every time, you waste time." Clara adjusted a set of files. "My father taught me that."

"He taught you well."

By evening, the workshop looked functional. Not perfect. But ready. Clara stood back and surveyed their work. Pride swelled in her chest.

This was theirs. Not her father's. Not the Blackwood family's. Theirs.

"We need a name," Nathaniel said. "For the shop."

Clara had thought about this. "Wren and Blackwood. Both our names. Equal."

"Not Blackwood and Wren?"

"No. Alphabetical order of our first names makes it fair. No one is first. No one is more important."

Nathaniel smiled. "Wren and Blackwood it is."

The next challenge was finding customers. Clara and Nathaniel both wrote letters. To people they knew. Former clients. Colleagues. Anyone who might need watch repair or custom work.

Most letters went unanswered. The few responses they received were polite but firm. People were uncomfortable. The scandal with the elder Blackwood was spreading. Pritchard's article would be published soon. No one wanted to be associated with the controversy.

"We're being shut out," Clara said after the fifth rejection. "People are afraid."

"They'll change their minds once the article is published. Once they see we were right."

"What if they don't? What if we're ruined before we even begin?"

Nathaniel took her hand. "Then we build slowly. Word of mouth. One repair at a time. We prove ourselves through our work."

"That could take years."

"Then it takes years." Nathaniel's voice was calm. Certain. "I'm not giving up. And neither are you."

Clara squeezed his hand. Drew strength from him. "No. Neither am I."

A knock at the door interrupted them. Clara answered it.

Mr. Pell stood outside. He looked older than Clara remembered. More tired. But his eyes were kind.

"Miss Wren. Mr. Blackwood. May I come in?"

"Of course." Clara stepped aside. "It's good to see you."

Mr. Pell entered and looked around the workshop. "So it's true. You've started your own business."

"We have," Nathaniel said. "Are you here from the factory? Did my father send you?"

"I came on my own accord. To see if the rumours were true. And to ask a question." Mr. Pell turned to face them. "Are you hiring?"

Clara and Nathaniel exchanged glances.

"We can't afford to pay much," Nathaniel said honestly. "We're just starting out. We have almost no customers yet."

"I don't need much. I've got my savings. A small pension. I'm not looking to get rich." Mr. Pell walked to one of the benches. He picked up a tool. Examined it. "I'm looking to work somewhere that values craftsmanship. Somewhere that cares about quality over quantity. Somewhere honest."

"The factory isn't honest?" Clara asked.

"It hasn't been for years. I've known that. But I was too afraid to leave. Too comfortable." Mr. Pell set the tool down. "But when I heard what you were doing. How you stood up to the elder Blackwood. How you're trying to make things right. I realised I couldn't stay there anymore. Not in good conscience."

Nathaniel stepped forward. "Mr. Pell, we would be honoured to have you join us. Your experience. Your reputation. It would help immensely."

"Then I accept." Mr. Pell smiled. "When do I start?"

"Whenever you want."

"Tomorrow, then."

Mr. Pell left with a promise to return the next morning. After he was gone, Clara turned to Nathaniel.

"That's good news. Mr. Pell brings credibility. People respect him. They'll trust our work more if he's here."

"And he's a good man. Skilled. Honest. Exactly the kind of person we want on our team." Nathaniel pulled Clara close. "Things are starting to fall into place."

"Slowly. But yes."

That evening, they worked late. Clara and Nathaniel sat at separate benches. Each working on different projects. But aware of each other. The quiet companionship felt natural. Comfortable.

Clara was designing a new escapement. Something more elegant than the standard factory models. She sketched. Erased. Sketched again.

Nathaniel looked up from his work. "What are you working on?"

"An idea. For our first collaborative piece. Something that shows what we can do together."

"May I see?"

Clara brought her sketches to his bench. Nathaniel studied them carefully. "This is beautiful. Efficient. Better than anything we made at the factory."

"It's just a sketch. I don't know if it will work in practice."

"It will. I can see the engineering. The precision." Nathaniel pulled out his own papers. "I've been working on a case design. Something distinctive. Different from the typical pocket watch."

He showed Clara his drawings. The case was slim. Elegant. With subtle engravings that suggested movement. Time flowing.

"It's stunning," Clara said.

"Your escapement. My case. We could combine them. Create something unique."

"A signature piece. To announce our workshop."

"Exactly." Nathaniel's eyes were bright with excitement. "We'll work on it together. Every detail. Every component. Make it perfect."

They spent the next hour discussing the design. What materials to use. What proportions. How to balance aesthetics with function.

Clara had never worked like this before. Collaboratively. With someone who understood her vision. Who challenged her. Made her ideas better.

"We should call it something," Clara said. "The piece. Give it a name."

"What about Hope? After everything we've been through. Everything we're fighting for. This watch represents hope. For the future. For justice. For us."

Clara felt tears prick her eyes. "Hope. Yes. That's perfect."

They worked until midnight. Refining the design. Planning the construction. When they finally stopped, Clara's hands ached. But she felt energised. Alive.

"I should go home," she said reluctantly. "My father will worry."

"I'll walk you."

They left the workshop together. The streets were quiet. Dark. Nathaniel stayed close to Clara. Protective.

"Thank you," Clara said. "For today. For all of this. For believing we could do this."

"I should be thanking you. You're the one who found the truth. Who pushed for justice. Who gave me the courage to stand up to my father." Nathaniel stopped walking. Turned to face her. "Clara, I need you to know something. This workshop. Our partnership. It's not just about business for me."

"I know."

"Do you? Because sometimes I worry that you don't see how much you mean to me. How much I... " Nathaniel stopped. Seemed to search for words. "You've changed my life. In ways I never expected. Ways I never thought possible."

Clara's heart raced. "You've changed mine too."

"Have I?"

"Yes. You've shown me that I don't have to hide. That my work has value. That I deserve respect." Clara moved closer. "And you've shown me what it means to care about someone. Truly care. Not just as a friend or a partner. But as something more."

Nathaniel's hand cupped her face. "Something more?"

"Yes."

He kissed her. Soft. Tender. Full of promise.

When they pulled apart, Clara was breathless.

"I love you," Nathaniel said. "I know I've said it before. But I need you to understand. This isn't just words. It's not just emotion. It's certainty. You're the person I want beside me. For everything. The workshop. The fight against my father. The future. All of it."

"I love you too. And I want the same thing. To build something together. Not just a business. But a life."

They stood in the quiet street. Holding each other. The world around them felt distant. Unimportant.

Finally, Nathaniel pulled back. "I should get you home. Before your father sends out a search party."

Clara laughed. "He probably already has."

They walked the rest of the way hand in hand. At Clara's door, Nathaniel kissed her once more. Then he waited until she was safely inside before leaving.

Clara entered the house. Her father was awake. Sitting in his chair by the fire.

"You're home late," he said.

"We were working. On a design. For our first piece."

"Our?"

"Nathaniel and I. We're making it together. Collaboratively. Each of us contributing our skills." Clara sat beside her father. "It's going to be special. Something that shows what we can do."

Her father studied her face. "You're happy."

"Yes. For the first time in a long time, I'm truly happy."

"That's good. You deserve happiness." Her father reached for her hand. "I'm proud of you. Of what you're building. The courage you've shown."

"Thank you, Papa."

"But be careful. The elder Blackwood won't give up easily. He'll keep fighting. Keep trying to destroy what you've built."

"I know. But we'll keep fighting too. And we're not alone anymore. We have Mr. Pell. And we have each other."

Her father nodded. "That's important. Partnership. It makes everything stronger."

Clara thought about Nathaniel. About their kiss. About the future they were building together.

Partnership. Yes. But also something deeper. Something that went beyond business. Beyond shared goals.

Love. Real love. The kind that made you braver. Stronger. Better.

Clara went to bed that night with hope in her heart. The workshop was ready. Their first piece was planned. Mr. Pell had joined them.

Things were falling into place. Slowly. But steadily.

And tomorrow they would continue. Working together. Building something new. Something honest. Something that honoured Thomas's memory and created a future worth fighting for.

Clara closed her eyes. In her mind, she saw the workshop. Saw herself and Nathaniel working side by side. Creating beautiful things. Proving everyone wrong.

It would not be easy. There would be challenges. Setbacks. Moments of doubt.

But they would face them together. As partners. As equals. As something more.

And that made all the difference.

Chapter Seventeen

T HE RUMOURS STARTED THREE days after Pritchard's article was published. The Birmingham Gazette had run the story on the front page. Bold headlines. Detailed evidence. Thomas's ledger exposed for all to see.

The response had been immediate. Some supported Clara and Nathaniel. Called them brave. Honest. Others were outraged. Defended the elder Blackwood. Said Clara and Nathaniel were troublemakers. Liars seeking attention.

But the worst damage came from whispers. Quiet words spread in pubs. In shops. At factory gates.

Clara heard them when she went to buy supplies. Two women standing outside the ironmonger's. They stopped talking when Clara approached. But not before she heard the words.

"Just a girl. No proper training. How can she call herself a watchmaker?"

Clara ignored them. Went inside. Bought what she needed. But the words stung.

That evening, Nathaniel returned to the workshop looking troubled.

"What's wrong?" Clara asked.

"I've been hearing things. About us. About our business." Nathaniel set down his bag. "People are saying we're frauds. That our claims about my father are lies. That we're trying to destroy a respected family for personal gain."

"Who's saying this?"

"Everyone. Or at least it feels that way. Former clients. Factory workers. Even people I thought were friends." Nathaniel's voice was bitter. "My father is spreading rumours. Quietly. Carefully. Making sure people doubt us."

Clara felt anger rise in her chest. "We have proof. Thomas's ledger. Inspector Hadley's testimony. The article laid it all out."

"Some people don't want to believe proof. They want to believe what's comfortable. What protects their world view." Nathaniel moved to the window. Looked out at the street. "My father has spent decades building connections. Friendships. He's calling in favours now. Asking people to question our story. To spread doubt."

"What kind of rumours?"

"That you're uneducated. That you can't possibly be a real watchmaker. That you seduced me to get revenge on my family for some imagined slight." Nathaniel's hands clenched. "And about me. That I'm mentally unstable. That I betrayed my family because I'm weak. Jealous of my father's success."

Clara sat down heavily. "This is worse than I thought."

"It's going to get worse before it gets better."

The next morning, Clara and Nathaniel were expecting a delivery. They had ordered gears from a supplier in Manchester. Precision parts needed to complete Hope. The shipment was supposed to arrive at dawn.

It did not come.

By noon, Clara was worried. "Where is it? The supplier confirmed the shipment three days ago."

"I'll send a telegram. Find out what happened."

The response came two hours later. The supplier was confused. The shipment had been delivered that morning. Signed for by someone at the Wren and Blackwood workshop.

"That's impossible," Clara said. "No one was here this morning except us. And we received nothing."

Nathaniel's face darkened. "Someone intercepted it. Took the delivery before it reached us."

"Who would do that?"

"My father. Or someone working for him." Nathaniel crumpled the telegram. "He's sabotaging us. Making sure we can't complete our work."

Clara felt panic rising. "We need those gears. Without them, we can't finish Hope. And we can't afford to order another shipment. We've spent almost everything on rent and supplies."

"I know."

"So what do we do?"

Nathaniel was quiet for a long moment. Then he said, "We improvise. We make do with what we have. We find another way."

"There is no other way. Those gears are custom made. We can't just substitute something else."

"Then we redesign. Adjust the mechanism to work with parts we already have."

Clara wanted to argue. To say it was impossible. But she looked at Nathaniel's face. Saw the determination there. The refusal to give up.

"All right," she said. "We'll redesign."

They spent the next two days working on new designs. Adjusting the escapement. Finding ways to make it work with standard parts. It was frustrating. Slow. But gradually, they found solutions.

Mr. Pell helped. His experience proved invaluable. He suggested modifications Clara had not considered. Techniques she did not know.

"You're very good at this," Clara said to him one evening.

"I've had a lot of years to learn." Mr. Pell set down his tools. "But you're better. You have instinct. Vision. You see things I never would."

"I don't feel like I'm better. I feel like I'm struggling. Barely keeping up."

"That's because you're doing something new. Something difficult. Of course it feels hard." Mr. Pell smiled. "But you're succeeding. Don't let doubt convince you otherwise."

Clara nodded. But the doubt was there. Growing stronger every day.

That night, Clara lay awake. Her mind raced. The rumours. The sabotage. The constant struggle to make ends meet.

What if she was wrong? What if she was dragging Nathaniel down? Ruining his life because of her own stubbornness?

Nathaniel had given up everything for her. His family. His inheritance. His position. And what did he have to show for it? A struggling workshop. Damaged reputation. An uncertain future.

Maybe her father had been right all those years ago. Maybe she should have stayed hidden. Safe. Maybe trying to be more than the world allowed was just foolish pride.

Clara got out of bed. Went downstairs to the workshop. She sat at her bench in the darkness. Surrounded by tools and parts. The familiar space that usually brought her comfort.

But tonight it felt oppressive. Like a reminder of all she had lost. All she had cost others.

The door opened. Nathaniel entered. He was dressed. Alert.

"I saw the light under the door. Thought I'd find you here." He sat beside her. "Couldn't sleep?"

"No."

"Me neither." Nathaniel was quiet for a moment. Then he said, "What are you thinking about?"

Clara hesitated. Then the words came out. Honest. Painful. "I'm thinking that maybe I made a mistake. Dragging you into this. Fighting your father. Starting this workshop. All of it."

"Why would you think that?"

"Because you've lost everything. Your family. Your money. Your future. And for what? A workshop that barely survives. A reputation that's been destroyed. A partner who..." Clara's voice broke. "A partner who can't even protect a shipment of gears."

Nathaniel turned to face her. "Clara, look at me."

She did. His eyes were serious. Intent.

"I haven't lost everything. I've gained something far more valuable." Nathaniel took her hands. "I've gained my integrity. My self-respect. A purpose worth fighting for. And you."

"But the rumours. The sabotage. Your father is winning."

"He's not winning. He's fighting. There's a difference." Nathaniel's grip tightened. "Yes, he's making things difficult. Yes, we're struggling. But we're still here. Still working. Still proving that we can build something honest. Something good."

"What if it's not enough? What if we fail?"

"Then we fail trying to do the right thing. That's still better than succeeding by being dishonest." Nathaniel moved closer. "Clara, I need you to understand something. I don't regret any of this. Not leaving the factory. Not fighting my father. Not starting this workshop with you. These past weeks have been the most meaningful of my life."

"Even though we're barely surviving?"

"Especially because we're barely surviving. We're building something real. Something that matters. And we're doing it together." Nathaniel cupped her face gently. "I love you. Not just as a partner. Not just as a collaborator. But as the person I want beside me for everything. The struggles. The victories. All of it."

Clara felt tears on her cheeks. "I'm scared. I'm scared we'll lose. That your father will destroy us. That I'll ruin your life."

"You won't. We won't let him." Nathaniel's voice was firm. Certain. "Clara, you're the strongest person I know. The bravest. You've faced down my father. Exposed the truth. Built this workshop from nothing. You don't give yourself enough credit."

"I feel like I'm drowning. Like everything is falling apart."

"I know. But you're not drowning. You're fighting. And you're winning. One day at a time. One piece at a time." Nathaniel wiped her tears. "We'll finish Hope.

We'll prove our worth. And we'll show everyone that we deserve to be here. That our work matters."

Clara wanted to believe him. But the doubt was so strong. So overwhelming.

"What if I can't do it? What if I'm not good enough?"

"You are good enough. More than good enough. You're brilliant." Nathaniel's voice was passionate. Intense. "Clara, I've worked with dozens of watchmakers. Hundreds, maybe. I've never met anyone with your skill. Your creativity. Your dedication. You're not just good. You're exceptional."

"You're biased."

"Maybe. But I'm also right." Nathaniel smiled. "Trust me. Trust yourself. We can do this."

Clara looked into his eyes. Saw the certainty there. The love. The absolute conviction that they would succeed.

Slowly, the doubt began to ease. Not disappear. But become manageable. Bearable.

"All right," she said quietly. "We'll keep fighting."

"Together?"

"Together."

Nathaniel kissed her. Gentle. Reassuring. Then he pulled her close. They sat in the darkness. Holding each other. Drawing strength from their connection.

After a long while, Nathaniel said, "Come on. Let's go back to bed. Get some rest. Tomorrow we'll finish Hope."

"Will we?"

"Yes. We will."

The next day, Clara and Nathaniel worked with renewed determination. They completed the redesigned escapement. Fitted it into the case. Adjusted. Tested. Adjusted again.

Mr. Pell watched. Offered advice. Made minor corrections.

By evening, the watch was finished. Hope. The first Wren and Blackwood creation.

Clara held it carefully. The case gleamed. The mechanism ticked steadily. Perfectly. It was beautiful. Everything they had imagined.

"It's done," she whispered.

Nathaniel stood beside her. "It's perfect."

Mr. Pell nodded approvingly. "This is fine work. Very fine. You should both be proud."

Clara felt pride swell in her chest. Despite everything. Despite the rumours and sabotage and struggle.
They had done it. They had created something beautiful. Something true.

"We need to show this," Nathaniel said. "Let people
see what we're capable of."

"How?"

"I don't know yet. But we'll find a way."

The answer came the next morning. A letter arrived.
From Pritchard. The journalist who had published
their story.

Clara opened it carefully. Read aloud.

"Dear Miss Wren and Mr. Blackwood. I've been
following your situation with interest. The public response to my article has been mixed. But I believe
there's an opportunity here. A chance to tell your story
more fully. To show people who you really are. What
you're really capable of. I'd like to propose a feature
article. An in-depth piece about your workshop. Your
work. Your partnership. If you're willing, I can arrange
for photographs. An interview. Perhaps a demonstra-
tion of your craftsmanship. This could help counter

the rumours. Give you a platform to prove yourselves. Let me know if you're interested. Regards, Pritchard."

Clara lowered the letter. Looked at Nathaniel.

"This is it," he said. "This is the opportunity we need."

"Are you sure? If we do this, we're making ourselves even more public. More visible."

"Good. Let them see us. Let them see what we've built. What we're capable of." Nathaniel's voice was confident. "We have Hope. We have our story. We have the truth. That's enough."

Clara thought about it. The risk. The exposure. The chance to finally prove themselves.

"All right," she said. "We'll do it."

Nathaniel smiled. "Together?"

"Always together."

They wrote back to Pritchard that afternoon. Agreed to the feature. Set a date for his visit.

That evening, Clara and Nathaniel sat in the workshop. Hope rested on the bench between them. A symbol of everything they had fought for. Everything they had built.

"Whatever happens," Clara said, "I'm glad we did this. Started this workshop. Fought for the truth."

"So am I."

"Even if we fail?"

"We won't fail. But even if we did, yes. I'd still be glad." Nathaniel took her hand. "Some things are worth fighting for. Even when the fight is hard. Even when victory isn't certain."

"Like justice for Thomas?"

"Like justice for Thomas. Like building something honest. Like you."

Clara squeezed his hand. "I love you."

"I love you too."

They sat in comfortable silence. The workshop around them felt like home. Despite the struggles. Despite the uncertainty.

This was theirs. Built on truth. On skill. On love.

And whatever came next, they would face it together.

Hope ticked steadily on the bench. A reminder that even in darkness, even in struggle, there was still possibility. Still potential.

Still hope.

Chapter Eighteen

T HE INVITATION ARRIVED A week after Pritchard's feature article was published. It came in a thick envelope. Formal. Expensive paper.

Clara opened it carefully. Read the elegant script.

"The Birmingham Society for Mechanical Arts requests the honour of your presence at their annual exhibition. We would be delighted if you would deliver a presentation on your work and your journey as a female watchmaker. The exhibition will be held on Saturday, the fifteenth of November, at the Town Hall. Please respond at your earliest convenience."

Clara read it twice. Then she set it down on the bench.

Nathaniel looked up from his work. "What is it?"

"An invitation. To speak at the mechanical arts exhibition."

"That's wonderful. When is it?"

"Two weeks from today." Clara's voice was flat. "They want me to talk about my work. My journey. In front of everyone."

Nathaniel moved to her side. "You don't sound pleased."

"I'm not sure I am." Clara picked up the invitation again. "This is... big. Public. Everyone will be there. Factory owners. Craftsmen. Important people."

"And you'll show them what you're capable of. What we've built together."

"Or I'll embarrass myself. Prove all the rumours right. Show everyone that I'm just a girl playing at being a watchmaker."

Nathaniel took her hands. "Clara, you know that's not true."

"Do I? What if I stand up there and my voice shakes? What if I forget what to say? What if they laugh at me?"

"They won't."

"How do you know?"

"Because I know you. You're intelligent. Articulate. Passionate about your work. When you talk about watchmaking, you're brilliant." Nathaniel squeezed her hands. "This is your chance. To tell your story. To show everyone who you really are."

Clara looked at the invitation. Her hands trembled slightly. "I don't know if I can."

"You can. I know you can."

That evening, Clara sat with her father. She showed him the invitation. He read it slowly.

"What do you think?" Clara asked.

"I think you're afraid."

"Yes."

"That's good. Fear means it matters. If it didn't matter, you wouldn't be afraid." Her father set down the invitation. "But you can't let fear stop you. Not now. Not after everything you've fought for."

"What if I fail?"

"Then you fail. But at least you tried." Her father's voice was gentle. "Clara, you've spent your whole life hiding. Working in secret. Pretending to be someone you're not. This is your chance to step into the light. To claim your place. Are you really going to turn it down because you're afraid?"

Clara was quiet. Then she said, "No. I'm not."

"Good."

Over the next two weeks, Clara prepared. She wrote notes. Practiced her speech. Went over it again and again until the words felt natural. Confident.

Nathaniel listened. Offered suggestions. Encouraged her when she doubted herself.

Lizzy came to help Clara choose what to wear. She brought three dresses. Simple but elegant. Nothing too fancy. Nothing that would make Clara look like she was trying too hard.

"This one," Lizzy said, holding up a dark green dress. "It's professional. Serious. But still feminine. It says you're competent without being intimidating."

Clara tried it on. It fit well. Made her look older. More confident.

"Perfect," Lizzy said. "You'll knock them dead."

"I hope so."

The day of the exhibition arrived. Clara woke early. Her stomach churned with nerves. She could barely eat breakfast.

Nathaniel arrived at noon. He wore his best suit. His hair was neatly combed. He looked handsome. Supportive.

"Are you ready?" he asked.

"No. But I'm going anyway."

They walked to the Town Hall together. The building was impressive. Grand. Stone columns. High ceilings. Clara felt small beside it.

Inside, the exhibition hall was filled with displays. Mechanical devices. Inventions. Timepieces. People moved between them. Examining. Discussing.

A man approached. Older. Well-dressed. "Miss Wren? Mr. Blackwood? I'm Dr. Harrington. President of the Society. Thank you for coming."

"Thank you for inviting me," Clara said.

"Your presentation is scheduled for three o'clock. In the main hall. We're expecting quite a crowd." Dr Harrington smiled. "Your story has generated considerable interest."

"How many people?"

"Perhaps two hundred. Maybe more."

Clara's stomach dropped. Two hundred people. All watching her. Judging her.

Nathaniel sensed her panic. He took her hand. Squeezed it gently.

"We'll be fine," he whispered.

They spent the next two hours walking through the exhibition. Looking at displays. Clara tried to focus. To distract herself from the growing dread.

But her mind kept returning to the speech. To the moment she would have to stand in front of all those people. Speak. Be vulnerable. Be seen.

At quarter to three, Dr Harrington found them again. "It's almost time. Would you like to come backstage?"

Clara nodded. She could not speak. Her throat was too tight.

Backstage, she could hear the audience gathering. Voices. Footsteps. The rustle of programmes.

Nathaniel stood close. "How are you feeling?"

"Terrified."

"That's normal."

"Is it?"

"Yes. Every speaker feels this way before going on. But once you start talking, it will get easier. You'll find your rhythm."

"What if I don't?"

"You will. I promise."

Dr Harrington appeared. "Ready, Miss Wren?"

Clara took a deep breath. "Yes."

They walked onto the stage. The hall was packed. Rows of seats. All filled. People standing at the back. Clara's vision swam for a moment.

Dr Harrington moved to the podium. "Ladies and gentlemen. Thank you for attending today's presentation. It is my great pleasure to introduce Miss Clara Wren. Miss Wren has recently gained recognition for her exceptional skill in watchmaking. But more than that, she represents something important. Something groundbreaking. A woman succeeding in a field traditionally reserved for men. Please welcome Miss Clara Wren."

Applause filled the hall. Polite. Cautious. Clara moved to the podium. Her legs felt weak. Her hands shook.

She looked out at the audience. Hundreds of faces. Some curious. Some skeptical. Some openly hostile.

Clara placed her notes on the podium. Looked down at them. The words blurred.

Then she looked up. Found Nathaniel. He was standing at the side of the stage. Watching her. He nodded. Encouraging.

Clara took a breath. Began to speak.

"Good afternoon. My name is Clara Wren. And I am a watchmaker."

Her voice was steady. Stronger than she expected.

"I did not start out as a watchmaker. I started as a watchmaker's daughter. My father ran a small shop in Birmingham. He taught me the trade. Not because he thought I would use it. But because I was curious. Because I wanted to learn."

Clara found her rhythm. The words came easier.

"When my father became ill, I took over the repairs. But I could not do it openly. Not as myself. So I hid. I signed my work as C. Wren. Let people assume I was a man. Because I knew that if they knew the truth, they would not trust me. Would not respect my work."

The audience was quiet. Listening.

"For years, I lived this way. In hiding. Pretending. Denying who I was. But it was not enough. I wanted more. I wanted to be seen. To be recognised. To have my skill acknowledged."

Clara paused. Looked out at the faces.

"Some of you may have read the recent articles about me. About my partnership with Mr. Nathaniel Blackwood. About the revelations regarding Blackwood and Sons. About the truth we uncovered."

A murmur went through the audience.

"I know there are rumours. Questions about my qualifications. My legitimacy as a watchmaker. Some say I am a fraud. That I cannot possibly have the skill I claim. That I am using my gender to gain attention. Sympathy."

Clara's voice grew stronger. More confident.

"To those people, I say this. I have trained for over ten years. I have studied every aspect of watchmaking. I have repaired hundreds of timepieces. I have designed and built mechanisms that others said were impossible. My gender does not diminish my skill. It does not make my work less valuable. Less real."

Some people in the audience nodded. Others frowned. But all were listening.

"I am here today not to defend myself. But to tell my story. To show you what is possible when we stop limiting people based on who they are. When we judge them on their ability. Their dedication. Their passion."

Clara gestured to where Nathaniel stood.

"Mr. Blackwood and I have started a workshop. Wren and Blackwood. We are creating timepieces that honour craftsmanship. Quality. Integrity. We are building something new. Something honest. And we are doing it together. As equals."

Clara picked up Hope from the podium. She held it up for the audience to see.

"This is our first creation. We call it Hope. Because that is what it represents. Hope for a future where talent matters more than gender. Where dedication matters more than tradition. Where anyone with skill and passion can succeed."

She set Hope down gently.

"I know that many of you are uncomfortable with the idea of a female watchmaker. That goes against everything you have been taught. Everything you believe about how the world should work. But I am here. I am real. And I am not going away."

Clara's voice filled the hall. Strong. Clear. Unwavering.

"I learned this trade from my father. A man who valued skill over everything else. Who taught me that good work speaks for itself. That quality cannot be hidden. Cannot be denied. I hope that someday, other fathers will teach their daughters the same. That other women will not have to hide. To pretend. To diminish themselves to be accepted."

She paused. Let the words settle.

"I am a Watchmaker's daughter, his apprentice. But I am also a master watchmaker. Both things are true. Both things matter. And I am proud of both."

Clara looked out at the audience one final time.

"Thank you for listening. For giving me this opportunity to speak. To be seen. I hope that my story, my work, will inspire others. To pursue their passions. To claim their place. To never let fear or tradition stop them from becoming who they are meant to be."

Clara stepped back from the podium. The hall was silent.

Then someone started clapping. Slowly at first. Then others joined. The applause grew. Filled the space.

Some people stood. Others remained seated. But most were clapping. Some enthusiastically. Some reluctantly. But clapping nonetheless.

Clara looked for Nathaniel. He was smiling. Pride evident on his face.

Dr Harrington returned to the stage. "Thank you, Miss Wren. That was quite remarkable. Are there any questions from the audience?"

Several hands went up. Clara's heart raced. But she nodded.

A man stood. Middle-aged. Well-dressed. "Miss Wren, how can you prove that you truly possess the skill you claim? Anyone can give a speech. But can you demonstrate your ability?"

Clara had expected this question. "Yes. I would be happy to demonstrate. If you have a broken timepiece, I can repair it. Here. Now."

The man hesitated. Then he pulled a pocket watch from his vest. "This watch has been broken for three years. Multiple watchmakers have tried to fix it. None succeeded. If you can repair it, I will believe your claims."

He brought the watch to the stage. Handed it to Clara.

She opened it. Examined the mechanism. The problem was immediately clear. A broken spring. Mis-aligned gears. Simple repairs. But requiring precision. Patience.

"May I borrow some tools?" Clara asked.

Dr Harrington provided a small toolkit. Clara sat at a table on the stage. The audience watched.

She worked carefully. Methodically. Replacing the spring. Realigning the gears. Cleaning. Adjusting. Testing.

Twenty minutes passed. Then she wound the watch. Held it to her ear. The ticking was steady. Perfect.

She closed the case. Handed it back to the man.

He examined it. Listened. His eyes widened. "It works. After three years, it works."

Applause erupted again. Louder this time. More genuine.

More questions followed. About her training. Her techniques. Her partnership with Nathaniel. Clara answered each one. Honestly. Confidently.

Finally, Dr Harrington ended the session. "Thank you again, Miss Wren. This has been most enlightening."

As people left, several approached Clara. Some wanted to congratulate her. Others wanted to commission work.

An elderly gentleman introduced himself. "Sir Edmund Grey. I collect fine timepieces. I would like to commission a watch from your workshop. Something unique. Exceptional. Money is no object."

Clara's eyes widened. "Of course. We would be honoured."

Two more patrons followed. Both requesting custom work. Both willing to pay generously.

By the time the hall emptied, Clara had three commissions. Enough work to keep them busy for months. Enough money to secure their future.

Nathaniel wrapped his arms around her. "You did it. You were brilliant."

"I was terrified."

"You didn't show it. You were confident. Articulate. Perfect."

Clara leaned against him. The adrenaline was fading. Exhaustion taking its place. "I can't believe people actually listened."

"They more than listened. They believed you. They respected you." Nathaniel pulled back. Looked into her eyes. "You changed minds today. Made people see what's possible. That's powerful."

Clara felt tears on her cheeks. Relief. Pride. Gratitude.

"Thank you. For standing beside me. For believing in me. For making all of this possible."

"You made this possible. All I did was support you."

They left the Town Hall together. The evening air was cool. Refreshing.

Clara felt different. Lighter. Like a weight had been lifted. She had stood in front of hundreds of people. Told her story. Claimed her place.

And they had listened.

Not everyone believed her. Not everyone supported her. But enough did. Enough to matter.

Clara thought about the commissions. About the future they represented. The security. The validation.

She thought about her father. About how proud he would be. About how far she had come from the girl who hid behind initials. Who was afraid to be seen.

"What are you thinking about?" Nathaniel asked.

"Everything. How different life is now. How much has changed."

"Are you happy?"

Clara smiled. "Yes. For the first time in a long time, I'm truly happy."

They walked home through the darkening streets. Together. Partners. Equals.

And Clara knew that whatever came next, she was ready. She had found her voice. Claimed her place. Proven her worth.

She was Clara Wren. Watchmaker. And she was not hiding anymore.

Chapter Nineteen

CLARA KNEW SOMETHING WAS wrong the moment she entered the house. The silence was too heavy. Too still.

She had been at the workshop all day. Working on Sir Edmund Grey's commission. When she returned home, the clocks were still ticking. But her father's chair by the fire was empty.

"Papa?" Clara called.

No answer.

Clara climbed the stairs. Her heart pounded. Each step felt too slow. Too loud.

She found him in his bedroom. In bed. His face was pale. His breathing shallow.

"Papa!" Clara rushed to his side.

His eyes opened. Slowly. With effort. "Clara. You're home."

"What happened? Why didn't you send for me?"

"I didn't want to worry you. You were working. I thought... I thought it would pass." Her father's voice was weak. Strained.

Clara touched his forehead. He was burning with fever. "I'm sending for the doctor. Right now."

"No. It's too late for that."

"Don't say that. The doctor can help. He can..."

"Clara." Her father's hand found hers. "Listen to me. We both know what this is. The illness has been coming for months. Years, maybe. This is just... the end of it."

Clara felt tears on her cheeks. "No. You're going to be fine. You have to be fine."

"I wish I could be. But some things we can't fix. No matter how skilled we are."

Clara sat on the edge of the bed. Held his hand. "I'm not ready. To lose you. I need more time."

"We never get as much time as we need. But we've had good years, you and I. You've made me so proud."

"Have I?"

"Yes. More than you know." Her father's breathing was laboured. Each word an effort. "You've become everything I hoped for. Everything I knew you could be. A true master of the craft. But more than that. A woman of courage. Of integrity."

"You taught me everything."

"I taught you the craft. But you learned the rest on your own. The bravery. The determination. The refusal to accept limitations." Her father smiled weakly. "That's all you, Clara. That's who you are."

Clara squeezed his hand. "I wish you could see what comes next. The workshop. The work Nathaniel and I are doing. All of it."

"I do see it. In my mind. In my heart. I know you'll succeed. I know you'll build something beautiful. Something that honours the craft. And honours yourself."

They sat in silence for a moment. Clara listened to his breathing. Irregular. Strained.

"There's something I want to show you," Clara said suddenly. "Wait here."

She ran downstairs. To the workshop. Grabbed Hope from its place on the shelf. Ran back up.

"Look," Clara said. She placed the watch in her father's hand. Gently. Carefully.

Her father held it. Examined it. His eyes brightened slightly. "This is... remarkable. The case. The design. This is your work?"

"Mine and Nathaniel's. Together. We call it Hope."

Her father opened the case. Looked at the mechanism inside. "Beautiful. Precise. This is master-level work, Clara. Better than anything I ever made."

"That's not true."

"It is. You've surpassed me. Taken everything I taught you and made it better. Made it yours." Her father closed the watch carefully. Held it against his chest. "This is perfect. A perfect symbol of what you've become. What you've achieved."

Clara felt tears streaming down her face. "I wanted you to see it. To hold it. To know that everything you taught me... it mattered. It wasn't wasted."

"Nothing between us was wasted. Every hour. Every lesson. Every moment." Her father's voice grew softer. "I'm so proud of you, Clara. So very proud."

"I love you, Papa."

"I love you too. More than words can say."

Her father's breathing grew more laboured. Clara stayed beside him. Holding his hand. Watching. Waiting.

As night fell, Lizzy arrived. Clara had sent word. Her cousin sat with them. Quiet. Supportive.

Near midnight, her father's eyes opened one final time.

"Clara?"

"I'm here, Papa."

"You'll be all right. You and Nathaniel. You'll build something wonderful. Something true."

"Yes. We will."

"And you'll be happy. That's all I ever wanted. For you to be happy. Safe. Respected."

"I am. Because of you. Because of everything you gave me."

Her father smiled. Peaceful. Content. "Good. That's good."

His eyes closed. His breathing slowed. Then stopped.

Clara felt the moment he left. Felt the absence. The stillness.

She sat there for a long time. Holding his hand. Unable to let go.

Finally, Lizzy touched her shoulder. "Clara. It's time."

Clara nodded. Gently, she placed her father's hand on his chest. Beside Hope. The watch that represented everything they had built together. Everything he had given her.

The funeral was three days later. A small service. Just Clara, Lizzy, Nathaniel, and Mr. Pell. Her father had not wanted a big affair. He had lived quietly. He would leave the same way.

They buried him in the churchyard. A simple headstone. Walter Wren. Master Watchmaker. Beloved Father.

Clara stood at the grave long after the others had left. The November wind was cold. But she did not move.

Nathaniel returned. Stood beside her. "How are you doing?"

"I don't know. Sad. Empty. But also... grateful. He died knowing I was safe. Knowing I had succeeded. That matters."

"He was very proud of you."

"I hope so."

"I know so. He told me once. Said you were the best thing he ever created. His greatest masterpiece."

Clara felt fresh tears. "He said that?"

"Yes. When I first came to commission work. Before I knew who you really were. He said his daughter was the finest watchmaker he had ever seen. That she would surpass everyone. Given the chance."

"And now he's gone."

"But his legacy isn't. You're carrying it forward. Making it real. That's what matters."

They stood in silence. Then Clara said, "We should go. There's work to do."

"Are you sure? We can take more time. The commissions can wait."

"No. My father wouldn't want me to stop working. He'd want me to keep going. To keep building. That's the best way to honour him."

They walked back to the workshop together. Clara felt the absence of her father. The space where he had been. But she also felt his presence. In the tools. In the knowledge he had given her. In the craft they had shared.

That evening, a messenger arrived. He carried a letter. Official. Sealed with the Blackwood factory crest.

Clara opened it. Read carefully.

"What is it?" Nathaniel asked.

"It's from the factory board. They want to meet with you. Tomorrow."

"Why?"

"It doesn't say. But it's marked urgent."

Nathaniel took the letter. Read it himself. "This is strange. I haven't been involved with the factory in weeks. Why would they contact me now?"

"Maybe it's about your father. About the scandal."

"Maybe."

The next day, Nathaniel went to the factory. Clara stayed at the workshop. Anxious. Uncertain.

He returned three hours later. His expression was complicated. Surprised. Almost disbelieving.

"What happened?" Clara asked.

"The board has forced my father to step down. He's no longer running the factory."

Clara's eyes widened. "What? Why?"

"The scandal. The publicity. Pritchard's articles. The evidence in Thomas's ledger. It all became too much. Clients were pulling orders. Investors were withdrawing. The board decided my father was a liability."

"So they removed him?"

"Yes. They gave him a choice. Retire voluntarily. Or be voted out publicly. He chose to retire." Nathaniel sat down. Ran his hand through his hair. "I never thought this would actually happen. I thought he was too powerful. Too entrenched."

"How do you feel?"

"I don't know. Relieved, maybe. That justice was done. That Thomas's death wasn't for nothing. But also... sad. He's still my father. Even after everything."

Clara moved to sit beside him. "I understand. He did terrible things. But that doesn't erase the connection. The history."

"The board also dismissed Basil. They discovered he'd been embezzling funds. Small amounts. Over years. He thought he was clever. That no one would notice. But when they started investigating my father's activities, they found Basil's as well."

"Good. He deserves to be held accountable."

"Yes. He does."

They sat in silence. Processing. Absorbing.

"There's something else," Nathaniel said. "The board asked me to return. To take over running the factory. To restore the company's reputation."

Clara's heart sank. "What did you say?"

"I said no. That I'm building something different now. Something better. With you."

Clara felt relief flood through her. "You're sure?"

"Completely. I don't want to run that factory. I don't want to be part of that world anymore. I want to be here. Creating things that matter. With someone I love."

Clara kissed him. Gentle. Grateful.

"Thank you," she whispered.

"For what?"

"For choosing this. For choosing us."

That weekend, Clara and Nathaniel visited the churchyard. But not to see Clara's father. Though they stopped there first. Paid their respects.

Then they walked to another grave. Older. More weathered.

Thomas Blackwood. Born 1848. Died 1872. Beloved Son and Brother.

Nathaniel knelt. Placed his hand on the headstone.

"I'm sorry," he said quietly. "Sorry I didn't see what was happening. Sorry I didn't help you when you needed it. Sorry it took so long for the truth to come out."

Clara knelt beside him. "He knows you tried. He knows you've honoured his memory. By standing up for what's right. By not letting his death be meaningless."

"I hope so."

"I know so." Clara touched the headstone. "Thomas, thank you. For trying to do the right thing. For standing up to corruption. For training with my father. For being brave when no one else was. We're going to make sure people remember you. Not just as the Blackwood son who died. But as someone who fought for justice. For truth."

Nathaniel looked at Clara. "Thank you. For helping me do this. For finding the truth. For giving me the courage to face it."

"We did it together."

"Yes. Together."

They stood. Nathaniel looked at the grave one last time. "I'm building something new now, Thomas. Something honest. Something you would have been proud of. Clara and I. We're partners. Equals. Creating timepieces that honour the craft. That honour you."

They walked back through the churchyard. The afternoon sun was low. Autumn leaves scattered across the paths.

"What now?" Clara asked.

"Now we expand. We've got three commissions. More work than we can handle with just the two of us and Mr. Pell. We need to grow."

"How?"

"A bigger workshop. More tools. Maybe apprentices. People who want to learn the craft properly. With integrity."

Clara thought about this. "A bigger workshop would be expensive."

"Sir Edmund Grey's commission will cover most of it. And the other patrons are paying well. We have the funds. If we're smart. If we plan carefully."

"Where would we go?"

"I've seen a property. Two streets over. Bigger than our current space. Room for multiple benches. Proper storage. Even a small showroom." Nathaniel's eyes were bright. Excited. "We could do real work there. Build something substantial. Something lasting."

Clara felt excitement rising. "Let's look at it. Tomorrow."

"Together?"

"Always together."

They returned to the workshop. The space felt different now. Smaller. Like they had outgrown it.

Clara thought about her father. About Thomas. About everything they had sacrificed. Everything they had fought for.

And she thought about the future. About what she and Nathaniel were building. Not just a business. But a legacy. A statement. Proof that change was possible. That courage mattered. That truth could win.

It would not be easy. There would be challenges. Setbacks. Moments of doubt.

But they would face them. Together. As partners. As equals.

Clara looked around the workshop. At the tools. The benches. The familiar space where everything had begun.

Soon they would leave this place. Move to something bigger. Better. But they would take the heart of it with them. The craft. The integrity. The love of good work.

And they would build something new. Something that honoured everyone who had believed in them. Everyone who had made this possible.

Clara's father. Thomas. Inspector Hadley. Mr. Pell. Even Pritchard, who had given them a voice.

They were all part of this story. This journey.

And the next chapter was about to begin.

Epilogue

Spring arrived in Birmingham. The smoke-filled skies gave way to occasional patches of blue. Trees budded. Flowers appeared in window boxes. And on a bright Saturday morning in April, Clara stood outside the new Wren and Blackwood workshop.

The building was larger than their previous space. Three times the size, at least. The front had large windows. Clean glass. A proper door with brass fittings.

And above it all, a sign. Freshly painted. Black letters on white.

Wren and Blackwood. Master Watchmakers.

Both names. Equal size. Equal prominence.

Clara felt tears prick her eyes. This was real. This was theirs.

Nathaniel stood beside her. He squeezed her hand. "What do you think?"

"It's perfect."

"Are you ready?"

Clara looked at the ribbon stretched across the doorway. Red silk. Elegant. Waiting to be cut.

Behind them, people gathered. More than Clara had expected. Fifty people, at least. Maybe more.

Some were former clients. People who had commissioned work. Who had supported them despite the scandal.

Some were artisans. Watchmakers. Craftsmen who respected what Clara and Nathaniel were trying to build.

And some were women. Young women. Older women. Women who had heard Clara's story. Who wanted to see what she had achieved. Who wanted to believe that change was possible.

Clara spotted Lizzy in the crowd. Her cousin beamed with pride. Next to her stood Mr. Pell. The old watchmaker smiled warmly.

Inspector Hadley had come. And Pritchard, the journalist. Both had played crucial roles in getting them to this moment.

"Thank you all for coming," Nathaniel said. His voice carried across the crowd. "Today marks a new beginning. Not just for Clara and me. But for what we believe the craft of watchmaking should be. Honest. Skilled. Open to anyone with talent and dedication."

He turned to Clara. "Miss Wren, would you like to say a few words?"

Clara's heart raced. But she stepped forward. She had learned to speak in public. To claim her place.

"Six months ago, I was hiding. Working in secret. Afraid to be seen. Afraid to claim my own work." Clara's voice was steady. Clear. "Today, I stand before you as myself. As Clara Wren. Watchmaker. And I am proud."

Applause rippled through the crowd.

"This workshop represents more than just a business. It represents possibility. The idea that skill matters more than tradition. That talent can come from anywhere. From anyone." Clara gestured to the sign. "My name is on that sign. Equally. Not as a token. Not as a novelty. But as a partner. As an equal. And I hope that someday, more women will have the same opportunity. The same chance to pursue their passion without hiding. Without fear."

More applause. Louder this time.

Clara picked up the scissors. Nathaniel stood beside her. Together, they cut the ribbon.

It fell away. The door was open.

People filed inside. Exclaiming at the space. The equipment. The clean, organized benches.

Clara had arranged everything carefully. The main room held three large workbenches. One for her. One for Nathaniel. One for Mr Pell.

At the back, two smaller benches. Waiting. Empty for now.

But not for long.

Clara moved through the crowd. Accepting congratulations. Answering questions. Showing people the workshop. The tools. The projects in progress.

Two young girls stood near the back. Nervous. Out of place.

Clara approached them. "Hello. I'm Clara Wren."

The older girl curtsied awkwardly. "Miss Wren. I'm Sarah. This is my sister, Anne. We read about you. In the newspaper. We wanted to see..."

"What a female watchmaker looks like?" Clara finished gently.

Sarah nodded. "Our father was a watchmaker. He died last year. He taught us some things. But no one will hire us. They say girls can't do this work."

"How old are you?"

"I'm fourteen. Anne is twelve."

Clara studied them. They had calloused hands. Ink stains on their fingers. The marks of people who worked with their hands.

"Can you read mechanical drawings?" Clara asked.

"Yes, miss. Our father taught us."

"And do you know the basic components of a watch movement?"

Sarah nodded eagerly. "The mainspring provides power. The gear train transfers it. The escapement regulates the speed. The balance wheel keeps time."

"Very good." Clara smiled. "Would you like to work here? As apprentices?"

Both girls' eyes widened. "Truly?" Anne whispered.

"Truly. We have two apprentice positions available. The pay is modest. But you'll learn properly. The right way. And when you're skilled enough, you'll be paid fairly. As watchmakers. Not as girls pretending to be watchmakers."

Sarah's eyes filled with tears. "We would be honoured, Miss Wren."

"Then it's settled. Come back Monday morning. Eight o'clock. Wear practical clothing. Tie your hair back. And bring your enthusiasm." Clara's voice softened. "I know what it's like. To want this and be told you can't. But you can. And you will. I promise."

The girls thanked her. Left with excited whispers and hopeful smiles.

Nathaniel appeared beside Clara. "New apprentices?"

"Yes. Sarah and Anne. Their father was a watchmaker. They know the basics."

"That's wonderful. The start of your legacy."

"Our legacy," Clara corrected.

The gathering continued for another hour. People examined the timepieces on display. Asked about commissions. Discussed designs.

Finally, the crowd thinned. People left with promises to return. To spread the word. To support the new venture.

By late afternoon, only Clara, Nathaniel, Mr. Pell, and Lizzy remained.

"It went well," Mr. Pell said. "Very well indeed. You should both be proud."

"We are," Clara said. "Thank you for being here. For supporting us."

"It's my honour. To be part of something honest. Something good." Mr. Pell stood. "I should be going. Let you young people celebrate properly."

Lizzy hugged Clara. "I'm so proud of you. Look at everything you've built."

"I couldn't have done it without you. Without everyone."

"Maybe. But you're the one who had the courage to try. To fight. To refuse to hide." Lizzy kissed her cheek. "I'll leave you two alone. You've earned some private time."

After they left, Clara and Nathaniel stood in the empty workshop. The space felt peaceful. Full of potential.

"Come here," Nathaniel said. "I want to show you something."

He led her to his bench. Picked up a small wooden box.

"I made this for you. For today."

Clara opened the box carefully. Inside was a watch. Smaller than their usual work. Delicate. Beautiful.

The case was silver. Engraved with intricate patterns. Flowers. Gears. All intertwined.

Clara opened it. The mechanism inside was exquisite. Perfect.

And on the inside of the case, words were engraved.

"To Clara, for all time."

Clara's breath caught. "Nathaniel, this is... beautiful."

"It's a reminder. Of everything we've built. Everything we've overcome. And everything we still have ahead of us." Nathaniel took the watch. Fastened it around Clara's wrist. "Time brought us together.

Time gave us this chance. And time will see us through whatever comes next."

Clara looked at the watch. At Nathaniel. At the workshop around them.

"I have something to ask you," Nathaniel said. His voice was nervous. Uncertain. "And I need you to listen. Really listen. Before you answer."

"All right."

Nathaniel took both her hands. "Clara, these past months have been the best of my life. Not because they were easy. They weren't. But because I spent them with you. Building something meaningful. Fighting for something that matters. Becoming the person I want to be."

Clara's heart raced. She knew what was coming. Had known for weeks, perhaps.

"I love you. Not just as a partner. Not just as a colleague. But as the woman I want to spend my life with. To build a future with. To grow old with."

Nathaniel took a breath. "I'm not offering to save you. You don't need saving. You're the strongest, most capable person I know. And I'm not offering to provide for you. You're providing for yourself. Building your own success. Your own reputation."

"Then what are you offering?" Clara asked softly.

"Partnership. True partnership. A life where we work side by side. As equals. Supporting each other. Challenging each other. Growing together." Nathaniel's eyes were intense. Sincere. "Clara Wren, will you marry me?"

Clara looked at him. At the man who had believed in her when others doubted. Who had stood beside her through scandal and struggle. Who had never tried to diminish her or control her. Who had offered her a sign with both their names. Equal.

"Yes," she said. "Yes, I'll marry you."

Nathaniel's face broke into a smile. He pulled her close. Kissed her. Deep. Passionate. Full of promise.

When they pulled apart, both were breathless.

"I should give you a ring," Nathaniel said. "That's traditional."

"I don't need a ring. I have this." Clara held up her wrist. The watch glinted in the afternoon light. "This is better than any ring. Because it represents us. Our

work. Our partnership. Everything we've built together."

"Are you sure?"

"Completely."

They stood together in their workshop. Surrounded
by tools and benches and the promise of the work to
come.

"When should we marry?" Nathaniel asked.

"Soon. But not too soon. We have apprentices to
train. Commissions to complete. A business to estab-
lish."

"So practical."

"Someone has to be." Clara smiled. "But yes. Soon.
In a few months, perhaps. When things are more settled."

"I can wait. As long as I know you're mine."

"I've always been mine," Clara corrected gently. "But
I'm choosing to share my life with you. There's a difference."

"I know. And that's why I love you. Because you
would never be content to be owned. To be dimin-
ished. You're too strong for that. Too proud. Too
yourself."

Clara kissed him again. "Thank you. For seeing me. For understanding. For never asking me to be less than I am."

"How could I? You're perfect as you are."

They sat together on one of the benches. Looking around the workshop. Their workshop. The foundation of their future.

"Do you think we'll succeed?" Clara asked. "Long term?"

"Yes. Not because it will be easy. But because we have the skill. The dedication. The integrity. And we have each other."

"That's enough?"

"More than enough."

Clara thought about her father. About Thomas. About everyone who had fought and sacrificed to make this moment possible.

"I wish my father could see this. Could know that his teachings led to something real. Something lasting."

"He knows. Wherever he is, he knows. And he's proud."

"I hope so."

They sat in comfortable silence. The afternoon sun slanted through the windows. Dust motes danced in the light.

Clara looked at the sign above the door. Wren and Blackwood.

She thought about the frightened girl who had hidden behind initials. Who had been afraid to be seen. Who had believed she had to diminish herself to survive.

That girl was gone. In her place was a woman. A watchmaker. A master of her craft.

A woman who had fought for her place. Who had refused to accept limitations. Who had built something beautiful from courage and skill and determination.

Clara Wren. Master watchmaker. Soon to be Clara Blackwood. But always, fundamentally, herself.

"What are you thinking about?" Nathaniel asked.

"Everything. How far we've come. How much has changed. How different my life is now from what I imagined it would be."

"Better or worse?"

"Better. So much better." Clara leaned against him. "I used to think success meant being allowed to work. Being tolerated. But now I know it means so much more. It means being seen. Being respected. Being valued. Not in spite of who I am. But because of who I am."

"You've taught me that too. That real success isn't about wealth or status. It's about integrity. About building something that matters. Something true."

Clara looked at her apprentice benches. Empty now. But Monday they would be filled. With Sarah and Anne. Two girls learning the craft. Following in Clara's footsteps.

It was the beginning of something bigger. Something that would outlast them both. A legacy of skill and courage and the refusal to accept limitations.

"We should go home," Nathaniel said. "Celebrate properly. Tell Lizzy the news."

"In a moment. I just want to sit here a little longer. In this space. Taking it all in."

"All right."

They sat together as the afternoon faded into evening. The workshop grew darker. The shadows longer.

But Clara felt only light. Only hope. Only certainty.

This was where she belonged. This was what she was meant to do. And this was the person she was meant to do it with.

Clara Wren. Watchmaker. Wife to be. Teacher. Pioneer.

She had claimed her place. Built her future. Refused to hide.

And whatever came next, she would face it. With skill. With courage. With love.

Because some things were worth fighting for. Worth risking everything for.

Truth. Justice. Love. Partnership. The right to be yourself, fully and completely.

Clara had fought for all of those things. And she had won.

Not perfectly. Not without cost. But she had won.

And that was enough. More than enough.

It was everything.

THE END

More from Helen

My latest – Her Mother's Last Lullaby: https://gen
i.us/MothersLastLullaby

Join me on Author Central to find all my titles!
Click here:
**https://www.amazon.com/author/helen_middle
-allmystories**

Printed in Dunstable, United Kingdom